EMMERDALE FARM · BOOK 11
LUCKY FOR SOME
A Star Original

All at once Steve's other hand came up, the one not holding Pip. It held the shotgun. 'Get inside,' he gasped.

'Now look here –'

But the sheer momentum of Steve's movement almost overbalanced the old man. He went back on his heels, into his shed.

At that moment Joe and Matt reached the foot of the steps. 'Steve!' Joe shouted. 'What the hell are you up to?' He was on his way up when Constable Edwards grabbed him from behind.

'He's got a gun,' he panted.

'I could see that,' Joe snorted, trying to pull free, 'but that's my grandad!'

'Keep back,' Edwards said, in the voice of authority that cannot be gainsaid. 'We don't want a murder done here ...'

Also by Lee Mackenzie in _Star_

EMMERDALE FARM   BOOK 11
LUCKY FOR SOME

Lee Mackenzie

Based on the successful
Yorkshire Television series
originated by Kevin Laffan

A STAR BOOK
published by
The Paperback Division of
W. H. ALLEN & Co. Ltd

A Star Book
Published in 1980
by the Paperback Division of
W. H. Allen & Co. Ltd
A Howard and Wyndham Company
44 Hill Street, London W1X 8LB

Printed in Great Britain by
Richard Clay (The Chaucer Press), Ltd,
Bungay, Suffolk

ISBN 0 352 30569 X

CHAPTER ONE

Mrs Acaster's arrival in Beckindale was like the coming of a storm. There was a forewarning, in the form of a letter to Dolly, which brought clouds to Dolly's brow.

'We ought to invite her to stay at Emmerdale, really,' Annie Sugden said with regret. 'Doesn't seem right, to have your mother putting up at t'Malt Shovel.'

'Malt Shovel's not so bad,' Matt put in.

'Not from the way Amos always goes on about it! He –'

'Of course he's always going to say t'Malt Shovel's inferior, Ma. But it's in t'list of approved accommodation –'

'It's best, really,' Dolly murmured. 'She's less likely to cause damage –'

'Nay,' Matt protested, but with a fond glance at his fiancée. 'She can't be that bad, love.'

'You don't know her! She's only here to cause trouble ...'

Dolly Acaster had had trouble enough in her relationship with Matt Skilbeck. A man from out of her past had done his best to wreck their love affair, but in his own quiet way Matt had seen him off. For perhaps five days he and Dolly had basked in the sunshine of true, secure affection – and then Mrs Acaster had replied to Dolly's letter about her engagement with the news (the warning, more like, according to Dolly) that she was on her way.

She proved to be a very good-looking woman in her early sixties: sharp, rather aristocratic features, well-groomed hair, slender feet in very expensive shoes, and a couple of matching suitcases at her side waiting to be picked up and carried. Carried, quite obviously by someone other than Mrs Acaster.

'Hello, Mother,' Dolly said in a very subdued tone as she came forward to greet her while the local bus ground away on its route.

Mrs Acaster held out her cheek to be kissed. Dolly dutifully kissed it. Mrs Acaster stood back and looked at the suitcases. Dolly picked them up.

'The Malt Shovel is just round the corner,' she ventured.

'I'd have thought you'd bring the hotel porter to carry the luggage, Dorothy ...'

'Er ... The Malt Shovel isn't exactly a hotel, Mother.'

'No ...' agreed Mrs Acaster, looking about at the village over the collar of her fur coat. 'I don't suppose the place runs to anything as grand as a hotel. Village inn, is it?'

'Something like that.'

'Hmm,' said Mrs Acaster, in a foreboding tone, and followed her daughter as she bore the two fine leather suitcases to the Malt Shovel.

Fred Teaker, landlord of the pub, was accustomed to offering accommodation to tourists in the dales, so that his welcome was warmer than anything the lady might have got from Amos Brearley of the Woolpack. Nevertheless, Amos was a bit put out when he learned that his bar-person's mother was putting up at the rival establishment.

'It's a very strange carry-on,' he complained to Henry Wilks, his partner. 'My staff having her mother to stay in Beckindale, and having her stay at the competition!'

'But you wouldn't have her here,' Henry pointed out.

'That's not the question –'

'It very much was the question when Dolly tried to suggest she should stay at t'Woolpack. You didn't let her finish the request.'

'That was because I took it for granted Dolly's parent would be offered hospitality at t'farm,' Amos remarked, lifting his chin in disdain. 'Funny thing, it seems to me, if they can't give a bed to a lady who's going to be their relative –'

'Now, Amos, you know very well that it's awkward there – it would have meant Dolly sharing with her mother –'

'I see nowt wrong with that. Natural, that seems to me.'

'But Mrs Acaster isn't the kind that likes to share a room, by all accounts, you see –'

'Well, then, why couldn't they put her up at Demdyke?'

'What, with Joe, in his bachelor squat?' Henry laughed. 'I gather Mrs Acaster is a very particular kind of lady –'

'Oh ... aye ... well, happen Demdyke wouldn't have been right ...'

'And because she's particular, it would have been much

6

more to her liking to be in a place like t'Woolpack,' Henry went on, rubbing it in. 'But there you are. What's done's done. She's at t'Malt Shovel. And if Fred Teaker gets t'chance to be friends with her and · Dolly, you'll mebbe find he'll entice your bar-person away from you.'

'Nay,' Amos muttered, 'Dolly'd never change over to t'Malt Shovel. Beneath her, is that.'

'Oh, so you agree Dolly's a cut above the rest as a barmaid?'

'I've always had a high regard for Dolly,' Amos said with great dignity. 'It's just that I don't like having female persons living in with me.' He didn't add that he'd furthered the romance between Dolly and Matt Skilbeck with the sole intention of keeping Dolly in his employ. He'd looked forward to a long, quiet engagement during which Dolly would continue to work for him, tidying and cleaning the inn, doing odd bits of washing for them, preparing meals which they would all share.

He'd been a bit taken aback to find Matt quite capable of sweeping Dolly off her feet. The wedding was being talked of as almost imminent. Amos hadn't learned yet whether Matt was prepared to allow Dolly to keep her job after their marriage – in Amos's book, husbands still decided whether or not their wives should work. Everything was in a state of dreadful uncertainty as far as Amos was concerned, so that when he heard that Mrs Acaster was considered 'difficult' he couldn't help half-hoping she'd cause the wedding to be postponed.

For as long as possible, he trusted. At least until he could wring a promise from Matt that he would allow Dolly to continue her employment.

But of course Amos couldn't say any of that aloud, and especially not to Henry Wilks. Henry was too fond of both Matt and Dolly to want any obstacle to their marriage. He, like everyone at Emmerdale, was fervently hoping that Mrs Acaster would be kind to the engaged couple.

Henry's feelings would have been very dashed if he could have heard what was being said in the bedroom at the Malt Shovel at that moment. Fred Teaker had just shown his guest into her room and brought up her cases, with a promise of a cup of tea to follow as soon as his missus had got it ready.

'Now, Dorothy,' Mrs Acaster said, taking off her mink

coat and folding it over a chair back, 'sit down. I want to have a serious talk with you.'

'Yes, Mother.' With nervous calm Dolly sat in the armchair. She met her mother's steely gaze and realised she was occupying the only comfortable chair. She sprang up. The other chair had the mink coat draped over it. Not daring to crush that fine garment, Dolly sat gingerly on the edge of the bed.

Her mother relaxed into the armchair for a moment, closed her eyes in thought, then sat up straight. 'You know why I've come here, don't you, Dorothy?'

'To ... to see me, Mother ... and meet Matt.'

'Hmm,' said her mother. It was a sound Dolly knew of old, full of disapproval and warning. 'I've come, Dorothy, to prevent you from throwing yourself away on a marriage that will bury you in the country with a man unworthy of you!'

That unworthy man, Matt Skilbeck, was coming home from the four-acre field for tea at that moment. His brother-in-law was tagging along behind much more slowly, in conversation with a teenage girl round whose thin shoulders his arm was slung in casual friendliness.

'I'll teach you to shoot if you want to, Pip,' he was saying in a teasing tone, 'but you know even as a kid at school you nearly fainted if you grazed your knee and made it bleed!'

'Nay, I don't want to,' she replied, shaking her head so that her brown hair tangled on his sleeve. 'I'd just like to come out wi' you on Sunday for a walk.'

'To get out of the house?' he asked with sympathy.

Pip Coulter made no response. They were almost at the gate of the farmyard. She hung back.

'Come on in,' Joe invited. 'Tea'll be ready.'

'No, thanks, Joe. Ma's expecting me.'

'You just said she'd gone to Hotten this afternoon.'

'She might have come back on the four o'clock bus ...' Pip's thin young face was red with embarrassment.

'And she wouldn't approve of you coming and having a cup of tea with us?'

She shook her head in dissent, but whether at the idea of her mother's disapproval or whether to emphasise that she couldn't come in with him, he wasn't sure.

'What about Sunday, then?' he continued. 'What'd she

8

say if she knew you were coming out wi' me?'

She looked up. Her greenish eyes flashed. 'I'm not going to tell her, am I?'

Joe was startled, then laughed. 'Well, I reckon you're old enough to go out for a walk on your own of a Sunday wi'out having to give chapter and verse.'

'It's all right with you, then?'

'Course it is.'

'Thank you, Joe.' To his astonishment she suddenly stood on tiptoe and brushed his cheek with her lips. 'You always were the kindest of the lads in school,' she said. 'See you tomorrow, then.'

She darted away into the gathering darkness of the winter day, while Joe went indoors divided between chuckles and concern.

'Come on, come on,' his grandfather scolded as he appeared. 'We're waiting for us teas! Where you been?'

'Just chatting,' Joe said, going to the sink to rinse his hands. 'I've been talking to Pip Coulter, Ma. She's right down in t'dumps.'

Annie Sugden set a shallow-dish pigeon pie on the table. 'Aye,' she said, as she returned to the stove for the vegetables. 'Pam Coulter's got one of her enthusiasms on again.'

'Not again?' old Sam said, pausing in the act of cutting into the pie. 'That girl's got less sense than one of these baked pigeons! What is it this time? Sacred Brethren? Chosen Disciples Sect? Total Immersion Believers?'

'It's nowt to joke about, Grandad,' Joe said as he took his place at table. 'Poor little mite, she's inventing excuses to get out of the house.'

'And be wi' you, I take it?' his grandfather inquired with a raising of his busy eyebrows. 'Another of your admirers, is she?'

'Gerron wi' thee! I've known her since she were a babby!' Joe glanced at his mother. 'She wouldn't come into t'house for a bite to eat, for fear her mother got to hear of it.'

'We're outside the pale again, as far as Pam Coulter's concerned,' Sam grunted. 'That's four times in the past five years, if I remember aright.'

Joe sighed. 'I thought Christianity was supposed to make folks kinder to each other?'

'Can't call it Christianity, the things Pam gets involved in,' said Sam. 'If you've noticed, it's allus summat that makes her feel superior to all the rest of us. Common Christianity's not good enough – she has to feel specially chosen so she can be gleeful while everybody else burns in He –'

'Now, Dad,' his daughter said with some sharpness, putting mashed potatoes on his plate. 'Common Christianity ought to urge us to be sorry for her, rather than make mock. Pam makes everybody's life a misery when she's got one of these salvation fits on –'

'Can't understand it,' Sam said. 'I mean, she weren't brought up C. of E., but chapel folk are sound enough in their own way. How's it happen she's allus getting caught up in these funny fads?'

'Potato for you, Matt?' Annie inquired, her spoon poised over the saucepan.

Matt made no reply.

'Matt?'

'Eh?'

'D'you want mashed potatoes?'

'Er ... no ... I mean, aye, I'll have some ...'

'She'll be back soon,' Joe said, in a comforting tone. 'She said she'd be back in time for tea –'

'Nay, she'll have to go straight to t'Woolpack if she doesn't come in a minute,' Matt said. 'It's opening time, nearly.'

'I don't know what you're so bothered about,' Sam remarked, swallowing a large hot mouthful so as to be able to offer this comfort. 'It's only Dolly's mother, you know. Not an ogre.'

'I wish she'd get back,' Matt muttered, absently shaking salt over his meal. 'She were right anxious about this meeting, I could tell.'

Joe had been sampling his pigeon pie in silence. He put out a hand to stop Matt's actions. 'Hold on, lad, you'll ruin it,' he opined. 'Just right, is this – doesn't need extra salt and pepper.'

'They were nice plump pigeons you brought home –'

'Plump on our barley,' Joe said.

'Nay, this time o' year, there's nowt for pigeons to crop in t'fields,' Sam said. 'Where would they get barley, eh? Even winter barley's just a few green shoots.'

'She said she'd be back by five,' Matt pursued, totally taken up by his own anxieties. 'It's gone that. I reckon she's had to go straight to t'Woolpack.'

'Well, only natural,' Joe said. 'A lass and her ma will have a lot to talk about, wi' a wedding in the offing.'

'Did you say you were going to take Pip Coulter out with you tomorrow, Joe?' Annie inquired.

'Reckon. Thought I'd go after rabbits Monday afternoon, so I'll spy out the land at stone-cross field – they come down from that old warren on Grey Top, I think.'

'Rabbit pie on Tuesday then, Annie?' Sam said with a pleased glance at his daughter.

'Should be, if Joe bags anything.'

'Hi! That's an insult! Have you ever known me go out and come back wi' nowt?'

This was a cue for Matt to remind Joe of one or two unsuccessful outings with the shotgun, but for once Matt didn't indulge in the straight-faced teasing that was his speciality. It was symptomatic of his anxiety about Dolly's mother that he didn't even seem to be aware of the opening Joe had left for him.

Nor was he aware of the eyes of his family turned on him at that moment. For the phone rang, and Matt leapt to answer.

Alas, it was the vicar, asking for Annie. When she picked up the receiver, Mr Hinton said guardedly, 'Annie, have you seen Mrs Coulter recently?'

Anne was taken aback. To have the vicar inquire so immediately about someone they'd just been discussing was odd, to say the least.

'Yesterday or the day before,' she replied. 'In the shop. Why?'

'How was she? Much as usual?'

'Er ...' She hesitated, not wishing to say that Pam Coulter had turned her back on her with pointed self-importance. 'We didn't actually speak, vicar. Why?'

'I can't discuss it now,' Mr Hinton said, unwilling in his turn to speak about a villager who was not one of his parishioners, more especially on the telephone, where some accidental link-up might make his words available to strangers. 'Could you drop by, do you think?'

'When, tomorrow?'

'We–ell ... this evening would be better, Annie.'

So it was urgent. 'I'll be there about seven,' she said. 'I

have some things to put in the village hall for Tuesday night's whist drive.'

When she sat down again at table the men were arguing about the resurgence of rabbits on Emmerdale land. That's to say, her father was arguing with Joe. Matt was still abstractedly pushing pigeon pie and mashed potato round his plate. 'Reckon I'll just stroll down to the Woolpack and see if Dolly's turned up there yet,' he said, rising.

'But Matt, you haven't eaten anything!'

'I'll get a pie or something in the bar.'

'But Matt –' Then Annie fell silent. What was the use of urging him to sit down and eat? He was too worried. Best to let him be off and away to see his girl. Poor Dolly. Actually trembling, she was, when she set off to meet her mother from the bus.

Dolly had just parted from Mrs Acaster on the worst possible terms. Mrs Acaster had announced that her sole purpose in coming to Beckindale was to break up the engagement. 'You never consulted me about it, Dorothy, and therefore I feel it's my duty to put an end to the whole thing before more damage is done.'

'Damage?' Dolly cried, her eyes going wide in her pale face. 'It's you that's doing the damage! Rampaging in here, telling me what to do! I've just got shot of Richard, Mother – I'm not having you trample all over Matt's feelings!'

'My dear girl,' her mother said, the words rich and impressive in her Tyneside brogue, 'I have no intention of trampling on anything.' She eyed her elegant feet and ankles by way of emphasising the absurdity of the notion. 'All I want is to extricate you from a situation where your own kind heart has landed you. You're too easily led, my dear. That's how you got embroiled with Richard – and, mind, you never let me know a word about *that* until it was much too late. This time I can save you from your own mistakes –'

'But it isn't a mistake, Mother!' Dolly cried, a bit wildly. 'I love him. Don't you understand?'

'But you loved Richard, if I remember rightly?'

'Oh!'

'You see, Dorothy? And this time it's all much worse. This time you've chosen a clodhopper. But don't you worry, I'll sort it all out and you'll thank me once you've come to your senses.'

Dolly, who was regarded by those who knew her as the epitome of commonsense and intelligence, was at a loss. She jumped up and began to fasten her jacket.

'And where do you think you're going?' her mother cried.

'To work, Mother! I'm expected at the Woolpack.'

'And that's another thing,' Mrs Acaster said. 'That's most unsuitable. No daughter of mine is going to be employed in the licensed trade.'

'All of a sudden it's unsuitable? You know very well I've had this job for nearly a year –'

'Yes, and left it already because it was wrong for you. Why you ever came back to it, I'll never know.'

'I came back because of Matt,' Dolly said, her hand on the door knob. 'I found I missed him, so I came back. And if you think, Mother, that anything you can say or do can make me give him up, you're backing a loser!'

'Dorothy!' her mother cried, scandalised at being defied. But the door had closed behind her.

Dolly hurried to the Woolpack with cheeks burning with shame and indignation at her mother's views. The idea of that overpowering lady giving Matt the benefit of her opinion of him filled her with dismay. Matt would never be able to withstand the self-important force of her mother's character. Dolly knew from experience how difficult it was to get even a word in when Mrs Acaster was in full flood. And she, Dolly, was quite loquacious. Poor Matt, who seldom used two words where one would do, would be swept away.

Of course Dolly didn't doubt that Matt loved her and would go on loving her. Yet a long and angry wrangle with her mother could only sour the situation. And already she and Matt had been through so much. Oh, God, wasn't it time for some peace, some happiness?

Amos greeted her with mild annoyance as she came into the inn. 'You're early,' he scolded. 'You woke me out of my afternoon nap, barging in like that.'

'I'm sorry, Mr Brearley.'

'Well, since you're here, you may as well give a polish to them sherry glasses. Mr and Mrs Folwood are bringing a party here before goin' on to dinner at the Feathers for their daughter's twenty-first.'

'Yes, Mr Brearley.'

'And if you're making a cup of tea, don't put any sugar in

mine. I've decided to give it up.'

'On a diet, Mr Brearley?' she said, trying to rouse herself to take an interest.

'Certainly not,' lied Amos. 'I read in this article in the *Courier* that sugar is like an addiction – and it's not my way to be addicted to anything, Miss Acaster, so I've decided not to take sugar in my tea.'

'What about coffee?'

'What about it?'

'Will you be taking sugar in coffee mid-morning when I make it?'

'Of course not. Didn't I just say I was giving up sugar?'

'Oh yes, I see. I'm sorry.'

'Miss Acaster,' Amos said with some asperity, 'I hope having your mother here on a visit isn't going to lead your mind astray on family enjoyment, because it bodes ill for t'work you have to do here.'

'No danger of me being led astray on family enjoyment, Mr Brearley,' Dolly said, in a tone that would have told anyone other than Amos she was very unhappy.

When Matt arrived, the Woolpack had just opened its doors. Matt was in danger of being in ahead of the pub's most faithful customer, old Walter. Amos, however, had sent Dolly into the kitchen to prepare the evening meal, so Matt had to idle away half an hour with an unwanted pint before she appeared in the bar. Amos then went to eat in the kitchen. Henry saw at once that the two young people needed to talk, so without being asked took the role of barkeeper while they settled in a corner.

'You're upset,' Matt said, taking one of her cold hands in his. 'I can tell.'

'Oh, Matt . . .'

'What's your mother been saying to you?'

To her horror, she felt tears welling up. 'She . . . she's dead set against us getting wed, love.'

'But why? She's never even met me –'

'Nor never will, Matt, the way she's going on. Almost as soon as she arrived she delivered an ultimatum – I was to pack up and go back to Darlington with her tomorrow. We had a fine old row about that, when she said she would rescue me against my will from my own mistakes.'

'But how can she be so sure you're making a mistake, Dolly?' Matt cried.

'Because ... because I was so utterly wrong about Richard,' she replied on a stifled sob.

'Oh, him,' Matt said, dismissing him with a little movement of the head. 'She's going to hold one mistake against you for the rest of your life?'

'Seems like it.'

'All right then, we'll just have to ignore her.'

'I can't do that, Matt. She's my mother.'

Gently he chafed her fingers between his own. 'You're cold, love. Have a rum or something to warm you up.'

'It's ... I just feel so ... I dunno – helpless, lost!'

'You're never lost while I know where you are,' Matt said.

All at once Dolly looked up and met his eyes. Tears sparkled on her long lashes. But a smile began to dawn behind the tears. 'Eh, Matt,' she sighed. 'Why do I get in such a coil, when I've got you?'

'I dunno,' he replied, teasing. 'I thought you had more sense.'

'Aye. I thought so too. But she's always had the power to make me feel ... sort of ... inefficient, inferior ... no, it's not that. It's just that nobody measures up to her standards.'

'Well, she's kind of high-powered, I suppose.'

'Oh aye. Company secretary. It's big stuff, Matt. She's used to dealing with the nobs. That's why it's so hard for her to understand life in Beckindale. She thinks we're a bunch of turnips, I'm sure.'

'Hi,' Matt said, 'ever seen a turnip lantern?'

'What? Oh, well yes, I suppose I have.'

'Even a turnip can get quite bright!'

Dolly broke into tremulous laughter. Matt, satisfied to have cheered her up, turned the conversation to their plans for next day which, being Sunday, was a day of less work for him. He was supposedly teaching her how to fish with rod and line. They talked about that until Amos reappeared and gave her a warning glance which summoned her back to her place behind the bar.

Matt then became aware he was hungry. The idea of a pie and a glass of beer didn't quite appeal. He said au revoir to Dolly and walked back to Emmerdale, confident that he'd find something to eat and the chance to think quietly about the problem of Dolly's mother. Annie, he recalled, would be out, at the Vicarage.

She was listening at that moment to a touchy problem the

15

vicar was putting before her.

'Mrs Coulter isn't one of my parishioners, you see, which makes it all the more difficult,' Mr Hinton said. 'Normally I'd go and have a chat with the parents. But in this instance it hardly seems appropriate.'

'Or worth the trouble,' Annie sighed. 'I'm afraid, Vicar, that Pam Coulter is going through one of her difficult phases again.'

Despite himself, Donald Hinton smiled. 'You say it is as if she were a kindergarten child.'

'You could almost say, she's never got past that stage,' Annie replied. Then, realising how unkind that was, she added hastily, 'Pam Coulter means well, you know. She wants to be good. I mean, really good, to live by the word of God ... But she seems to me to find His word harsh and unbending. And that poor little daughter of hers has to live as if she were in a home for delinquent children.'

'I see. So that's why she wants to leave home.'

'It's very understandable. And with you having given Dolly a home –'

'But very unwillingly, Annie!'

'Pip Coulter isn't to know that. All she knows is that Dolly used to have a room here and only left to come to Emmerdale because she's going to marry our Matt. From Pip's point of view, you have a room to let.'

'Poor child,' Hinton said. His square, dark face was sad. 'I could see she was very distressed when I turned her down. She ... er ... she more or less accused me of being scared of her mother.'

Annie looked at him, and they both smiled. 'Well,' Annie admitted, 'there's something about Pam Coulter that does strike terror into men's hearts. Her husband, Will Coulter – do you know him?'

'The man who plays in the bowls team, with the green shirt?'

'That's him. I never can understand why she hasn't made him give up bowls. I'm sure she could find something against it in the Bible if she tried. I remember Will when we were at school. A likely lad if ever there was one. But she's ... she's sort of tamed him ...'

The vicar allowed a moment to go by before he went back to the main point. 'What I was wondering, Annie, was if you

16

could go and speak to Mrs Coulter?'

'Me?'

'Is it such an alarming prospect? I'm sorry. But from all I can gather, she won't even let me in the house if I call.'

'No, you're right,' Annie agreed. 'At the moment, Church of England clergymen are as good as servants of the devil –'

'As bad as, you mean.'

'Aye. Daft, isn't it?'

'I thought she might be more open to something coming from you, Annie. She respects you.'

'I don't know so much ...'

'Everyone respects you, Annie,' Hinton said quietly. 'That's not an empty compliment. I'm sure Mrs Coulter will listen to anything you say.'

'Not if I'm asking her to go a bit easier on Pip. And that's what you want me to say, isn't it?'

Donald Hinton blew out his cheeks in despair. 'How can it come about that a nice child like Pip Coulter is driven to come to me – almost a complete stranger – and ask to be taken in? What kind of a home must it be that pushes her to such a step?'

'It's bad,' Annie agreed, nodding. 'I just wish ...'

'What?'

'That you could have taken her, vicar.'

'That was impossible, Annie. The child is still a minor.'

She started in surprise, then coloured. 'Of course. She's only sixteen.'

'Quite so. I regard it as wrong to separate a child from its parents if it can be avoided, but all the more so in this case, where sectarian bitterness seems to come into it. And somehow a girl of that age is felt to be in such extreme danger where a man is concerned – can't you just see the headlines in the newspapers if Mrs Coulter were to make a fuss? "Country Vicar takes Girl into his Home" – no, no, Annie. Even if it were a teenage boy, it would be dicy. And to tell the truth –' and the vicar's shoulders sagged – 'I just don't think I could have done any good even if I had taken Pip into sanctuary. I ... don't really understand young people. It's one of my greatest lacks as a priest.'

'That's not so, Mr Hinton –'

'It is, Annie. I'm good with old people and the generality of my congregation. But anyone under the age of twenty tends to be a mystery to me. And they know it. So they don't take to me.'

Annie was about to say, 'Joe likes you.' Luckily she checked herself in time, for the clumsiness of that comfort was equal to its artificiality. She wasn't really sure that her younger son liked Mr Hinton. He respected him, true. But he probably felt for Hinton something far short of the friendship he'd had for Mr Hockley, his predecessor. Hockley had had a warmth, an energy, that Donald Hinton lacked. It might be that Hinton made up in wisdom what he lacked in outgoing friendliness, but in Annie's experience young folk weren't apt to recognise wisdom when they saw it.

Little Pip Coulter, for instance. She would think Mr Hinton cowardly when he refused her a home in the vicarage. It was too much to expect her to see that he was preserving her from worse things by his refusal.

'I hate to put the task on to you,' the vicar was saying as she thought it over, 'but if you could have a word with Mrs Coulter, tell her that her own daughter is so unhappy she wants to leave home . . . ?'

'She's not going to take any notice of me, Mr Hinton.'

'She may. After all, you've been acquaintances all your lives. You say Joe was at school with Pip –'

'She was in t'baby's class when he was about due to leave school. They're not exactly close. But he's fond of her.'

'That gives you at least some leeway. More than I have, don't you agree? I come from "the opposition" – the established church which she despises. She might even think I'm try to recruit Pip for my congregation!'

'And that would never do,' Annie agreed with a wry smile. 'All right, vicar. But I fancy I'll be wasting my time.'

Fastening up the fur collar of her coat against the chill night air, she set off down Vicarage path and into the High Street. At the corner of Becket Lane, where the lights of the Malt Shovel were glowing, she saw a well-dressed woman strolling as if to take the air before her evening meal. She was a stranger to Annie, but in the dim light of the High Street lamps she could glimpse a rather good mink coat and a head scarf of the kind you saw in the windows of high-class boutiques. Annie said a 'Good evening' as she hurried by. The stranger didn't answer – but then, strangers often didn't. One of the things Annie found odd about townsfolk was the way they never uttered a greeting in the street.

Annie knocked at the door of the Coulters' house. It was a pleasant little dwelling in one of the turnings behind the row which contained the village shop. Will Coulter was a successful man in his way, a carpenter and joiner much in demand when a cottage was to be restored and refurbished.

It was Will himself who opened the door. 'Oh!' he said in surprise on seeing Annie. 'Annie! Fancy it being you! We were expecting Mr Pangrave –'

'Who's Mr Pangrave?'

'The preacher. He's coming to give an evening of prayer and penitence with us and a few friends. I, er, I don't think I better ask you in, Annie.'

'Who is it, Will?' called Pam Coulter's voice from inside the house.

'It's er, nothing, my dear,' Will said in alarm.

'Then close the door and come back! I need help shifting these chairs.'

'I ... er ... I'd better go,' Will said in a whisper.

'Are you coming, Will?' Mrs Coulter called, and then appeared at his elbow in the doorway. At sight of Annie she drew up short.

'Ah!' she gasped. And then, very tart, 'You may well say it's nothing! Come in and close the door, Will.'

'Just a minute,' Annie said, finding her voice in the face of this bout of bad manners. 'I came on purpose to speak to you, Pam. Please spare me a minute or two.'

'We haven't time to waste on the likes of you, Annie Sugden. Our time must be given to those who can be saved.'

'What?' Annie gasped. 'No, wait! It's about Pip that I want to talk –'

It almost seemed as if this was the worst thing she could have said. Pam Coulter, small, prim and dark, bristled like a hedgehog.

'I'll thank you not to take my daughter's name into your mouth,' she snorted. 'She's no concern of yours!'

'But Pam, if you'd just let me speak –'

'"God is in heaven, and thou upon earth, therefore let thy words be few!"' quoted Pam Coulter. 'Ecclesiastes Five, Two. And that's all I have to say to you, Annie Sugden.'

'Well,' flashed Annie, 'remember Ecclesiastes Seven, Six-teen – "Be not righteous overmuch"!'

She regretted the riposte as soon as she'd uttered it, for the reaction was the last thing she wanted. Pam Coulter closed the door in her face.

Very depressed at her own lack of success, she went back to the vicarage to report to Mr Hinton. When she passed the corner of Becket Lane she didn't recall the woman in the mink coat, who in fact had gone indoors to have the meal she called dinner and Fred Teaker called tea. She'd managed to delay it until seven o'clock despite the fact that Mrs Teaker had got it ready at six. Mrs Acaster wasn't the type to be bullied by a country landlady.

The food proved to be surprisingly good. The landlady of the Malt Shovel had no pretensions to haute cuisine but knew how to stew steak and boil potatoes without spoiling the flavour. For dessert there was fruit cake, which wouldn't have been Mrs Acaster's choice but which was good of its kind.

After eating in the little snug at the back, Mrs Acaster came into the bar for an after dinner drink. She fancied a Grand Marnier, and was agreeably surprised when Fred Teaker not only supplied it, but in the right glass.

She was sipping it with approval, and thinking over how to get her daughter out of the clutches of this country bumpkin who'd captured her, when a quiet-looking young man asked if he might share her table.

'By all means,' she said grandly, inclining her head.

'Cold weather,' he said, unfastening his anorak.

'I daresay it's always colder out in the country than in the town,' she allowed.

'You're from the city?' he asked. And then, with admiration, 'But of course you are.'

She smiled. It pleased her to be recognised as a cut above the other women hereabouts.

'Can I buy you another?' he inquired. 'What is it – liqueur brandy?'

'Thank you. Grand Marnier.'

'Fred, another of the same, and a half of dark.'

'That's very kind of you.'

'Not a bit,' he said. 'I want to talk to you, as it happens. My name's Matt Skilbeck.'

Mrs Acaster set down her glass with a jolt. She stared at Matt through her ornate spectacles. 'Skilbeck?' she gasped.

'That's right. And you're Mrs Acaster.'

'Yes. Yes, I am. But how did you know?'

'Because you're the only woman in Beckindale who could be Dolly's mother. She told me you were a high-up in business – and that's you to a T.'

Despite herself, Mrs Acaster was flattered. But she steeled herself against it. 'It's very dishonest to come here inveigling yourself into my company –'

'I didn't inveigle. I offered you a drink and you accepted. Besides, you wouldn't have spoken to me otherwise. Now would you?'

'You're dead right,' she snapped, rallying. 'And I'm not going to speak to you now!'

'Why not? Scared of me?'

'Scared? Of you? You must be joking!'

'I can't think of any other reason you won't discuss the situation. From what Dolly tells me, Mrs Acaster, you're a smart woman. You must have seen business situations that reached a deadlock. You never get to a solution of a deadlock if you don't talk.'

'Ha,' she said. 'Quite right. But I don't want a solution. I want a withdrawal. I intend to take Dolly away from here, and talking won't help.'

Fred came with the drinks. Matt let him set them down before he spoke again. 'I'll tell you something, Mrs Acaster,' he said. 'If you don't talk to me, you'll be the loser.'

'What? You dare to suggest that I couldn't talk sense into Dolly?'

'How can it be sense?' Matt demanded. 'It seems to me more like prejudice. Until the minute I told you my name, you were nice as pie to me this evening – now weren't you?'

'I'm always polite –'

'Let's go on that way, then. I want to be polite to you. I want to be friends, in fact. But if it comes to a show-down atween the two of us, Mrs Acaster ... I'd be the winner.'

'Don't flatter yourself, young man.'

'It's not a question of flattery. Dolly loves me. An' I love her. That's the top and tail of it.'

Mrs Acaster flinched. He said it with so much certainty that he shook her for a moment. 'Well, even so,' she insisted, 'what kind of life do you think you can give her, tell me that? So far as I can gather, you're a farm labourer –'

To her annoyance, Matt laughed.

'Eh, missus, you're an old-fashioned one, aren't you? Farm labourer? Even if it was true, what's so bad about that? Settled job, rent-free house, chance to specialise in livestock or agriculture or crop-maintenance or farm machinery ... But,' he went on as Mrs Acaster opened her mouth to protest, 'as it happens I'm a partner in Emmerdale Farm Limited.'

'Partner, are you? Partner of nothing, judging by the land I saw from the bus. Seems to grow nothing but stones.'

'I might say, if I wanted to be nasty, that just shows your ignorance. This isn't arable land. We're a livestock farm — certified milk herd and prize-winning sheep. We make a good living — nothing fancy, but it's all right. But that's not the point. It just happens to be what I do, and I am going to marry Dolly.'

'Over my dead body!'

He smiled and shrugged. 'Don't tempt Providence,' he said.

'Look here, young man! Dolly has made one mistake already and I intend to see she doesn't make a second. She is not going to marry you. Cows and sheep —! It's ludicrous! She is coming home to Darlington with me.'

'No she's not. And if you're as bright about business as she says you are, you must know when you're beaten.'

Mrs Acaster's colour had risen, and her bespectacled eyes were snapping with ire. 'Let me tell you, you thickheaded country bumpkin, the day I allow myself to be beaten by a yokel will be the day of the Last Trump!'

If she had expected to see Matt lose his temper, she was disappointed. 'Go ahead,' he said. 'Sticks and stones will break my bones, but names will never hurt me. I've been insulted by experts, lass.'

Matt was thinking of his passage of arms with Richard, the man from whom he had had to rescue Dolly a few weeks ago. Richard had had a tongue like a rapier. Nevertheless, Matt had held his own against him, and it was this which had given him the courage to beard Mrs Acaster in her den. Sitting at home at Emmerdale over a piece of Annie's pigeon pie and a cup of double-strength tea, it had come home to him that he had nothing to be afraid of. Dolly loved him, he loved Dolly. Mrs Acaster could do nothing to change that. He, Matt Skilbeck, held all the aces.

The problem was to convince his future mother-in-law of that fact.

Mrs Acaster had the strange sensation that she was losing this fight. She had meant to avoid ever speaking to this young man, and if she had to, she had expected to wipe the floor with him. Instead he was sitting across the table from her looking calm and controlled, whereas she was beginning to feel a little frayed around the edges.

Desperation drove her to a move she knew was wrong. 'You don't know, I suppose, that Dorothy was involved in a foolish relationship which resulted in an unwanted child?'

If she thought he would go pale, she was disappointed.

'Unwanted?' he said. 'I got the impression she wanted him very much. But since nobody gave her any help, she let him be adopted.'

'She ... told you?' gasped Dolly's mother.

'Aye. But don't think you're the first to try to use it as a weapon. He did, too – that Richard character.'

'Richard? You've met him?'

'I had that pleasure.'

There was a long pause.

'You don't mind that my daughter has a ... a past?'

'I've got a past too.'

'Not like hers.' She studied him. 'You were married, though.'

'Did she tell you that?'

'No. There's something about you that tells me.'

'I was married. I had two children. My wife died of a brain haemhorrage and the children were killed in a train crash.' He hesitated. 'You see, Mrs Acaster? I'm not exactly a teenage wonder. I know Dolly could do better than a widower with a part share in a farm. But I happen to be what Dolly wants, and she ... well, she's everything I've thought I'd never find again.'

'Hm ...' She picked up the Grand Marnier she hadn't touched so far, looked at it, then suddenly held it up. 'I've decided I like you, Matt Skilbeck.'

'Thanks,' Matt said with some dryness.

'Against my will, mind!'

'Sorry about that.' He offered her his hand and they shook. 'Now', he said, 'let's go where the company's better, if not the drinks.'

'Where?' she asked, puzzled, but getting up at his urging. 'T'Woolpack, where else? Let's tell Dolly that hostilities have ended.'

She pulled back as he was ushering her to the door. 'Mr Skilbeck, hostilities will never cease if you insist on calling my daughter by that terrible name. I named her Dorothy.'

'You call her that, then. I love her whatever name she has.'

Bemused, Mrs Acaster allowed herself to be steered out of the Malt Shovel. If this was a country bumpkin, he seemed to have the knack of getting the better of her no matter what ploy she tried!

They walked through the village, chatting easily. Neither of them saw the slight figure sheltering from their sight in the shadows of the village hall.

It was Pip Coulter, supposedly gone to bed at her mother's orders after being less than polite to the visiting preacher. She had climbed out of her bedroom window because the bedroom door was locked. But there was nothing unusual about that – she'd climbed out before and would do so again.

She was on her way to meet her lover.

CHAPTER TWO

Joe went shooting as he'd promised. But Pip Coulter didn't turn up to share the outing. He wasn't particularly perturbed, because there had been nothing firm about the date. He'd felt she only wanted to get out of the house, out of her mother's reach.

Happen those two had got on friendlier terms for the moment. Or – more likely – the whole family was being forced to go to some weird meeting in Connelton or Hotten or somewhere.

Joe bagged a couple of rabbits quite early and contented himself with walking with the gun broken open and over his arm. He was always careful with firearms. He was happy enough on his own but quite pleased when young Steve Hawker joined him on the slopes of Grey Top.

'See you got a couple,' Steve said.

'Yeah, not bad.' Joe let him fall into step with him. 'Not working today?'

'Got the sack last week,' Steve said in a weary voice.

He was a handsome lad, seventeen years old but tall for his age. In a way he was a justification of all Mrs Acaster's fears about life in the country, for Steve was clever and ambitious, but handicapped by a father who spent his entire day handicapping horses and watching the racing when it was on TV. No encouragement, no help, was ever held out to him. He had had a dead end job in a chicken packing factory some miles out towards Bradford, entailing a long cycle ride night and morning. To tell the truth, he wasn't sorry to have been handed his cards the previous week on the grounds – agreed by his shop steward – that he was unreliable and stroppy.

Joe muttered something sympathetic. 'Doesn't matter,' Steve said, 'I didn't like the job anyway. Rather do what you do – please myself.'

'Huh!' Joe said, pulling down the sides of his mouth. 'You should try it. I'm only out shooting until it's time for milking. Light's going,' he added, turning back towards the track leading to where he left the Landrover.

Steve walked with him, huddling himself in his ex-army camouflage jacket against the rising wind. 'Always put it there, do you?' he asked as Joe carefully stowed the shotgun away in folded sacking between the front seats.

'Aye, when I've got it outdoors. Can't be too careful wi' guns.'

'Not loaded, though, is it?'

'I should hope not!' Joe put the cartridges he'd emptied out into the sack with the rest, and gestured to Steve. 'Want a lift anywhere?' he asked.

'I'll come down to t'farm with you.'

'Not going home?'

'Nah,' sighed Steve. 'What's there to go home for?'

In silence Joe put the Landrover in motion and they drove over the stony ground towards the stony-cross field and the field gate.

'A shotgun's a sort of limited firearm, isn't it?' Steve said.

'Limited? Limited to what?'

'I mean, it's only scatter fire. Doesn't kill folk.'

'Don't you believe it,' Joe said sharply. 'A shotgun's not for fun. It kills rabbits, it can kill a man.'

Steve made a movement of his head that seemed to reject that. 'I was reading in t'paper – about a bank raid, I think – how they saw off the end so as to scatter fire. Means you'd have to be quite close to someone to do 'em any harm.'

Joe shook his head with emphasis. 'They saw off t'barrel so they can keep 'em hidden easier – in a jacket, like. Nowt to do with not harming folk. Right enough, it scatters the shot but that doesn't make the shot any less lethal.'

'Oh,' Steve said. 'I see.'

Joe's thoughts were elsewhere. 'I thought to see young Pip up on the moor today. Said she'd like a walk wi' me if I were shooting.'

'Oh aye?' Steve said, carefully, facing straight ahead.

'Didn't happen to see her as you came up t'track?'

'Nope.'

'You know Pip Coulter, don't you? Little slight lass.'

26

'Oh aye, I've seen her about.'

'Um,' said Joe. 'I'd drop by her house and ask if she's okay, only that mother of hers is a pain in the neck.'

'You can say that again,' Steve said, with so much feeling that Joe glanced at him in surprise. 'I only mean,' Steve amended quickly, 'she glares at you if you go past whistling a pop song.'

'Does she? I don't go past her house much. Ma says she's not easy to talk to – and if Ma says it, it means she's a tartar because Ma never speaks ill.'

Steve looked as if he were about to say that Mrs Coulter was impossible to talk to, but pressed his lips together.

At the entry to Emmerdale's lane, Steve jumped down, nodded his thanks, and strolled away. When he reached the traffic road, he walked along it for a while then climbed the field wall. For a few yards he walked along the bank of a brook, a tiny stream hardly more than a drainage channel. By and by it joined a marshy path that had once been a stream until it was diverted for the mill race. It was overgrown with bramble and scrub willow but he forced his way up the muddy track until he reached firmer ground. Here there was an old footpath, overgrown too, but walkable. After about half an hour's walk from Emmerdale he came to the remains of an old stone cottage, the roof fallen in, what few slates remaining caked with moss. He whistled softly – two long notes, two short.

A girl came out of the ruin. She flew to him, throwing herself into his arms. 'Oh, Steve! You've been gone such a long time!'

He kissed her gently, holding her with pride and tenderness. 'All right, Pip, now all right. I'm here. Were you getting lonesome?'

'I was scared!' she whispered. 'I could see it was getting darker and the trees ... they sort of seemed to be closing in on me ... And funny noises ... creaks and scuttles ...'

'That'll be the mice,' he said. 'I bet they're surprised to have us in their house! Nobody been here for fifty year or more, I bet.'

'Come in,' she said. 'I got some coffee going.'

'How come?' he asked, putting his arm around her and accompanying her into the ruin. 'What did you use?'

'Well, I took some instant coffee from Mother's pantry

27

before I left the house, and I found an old saucepan and got water from the spring.'

'But heating it?'

'I lit a fire –'

'You mustn't do that!' he cried. 'They'll see the smoke –'

'Oh no, Steve. It's ever such a little fire of dry sticks. The smoke can scarcely creep out through the holes in the roof.'

She smiled as she said it, and her pale little face was transformed. Steve hadn't the heart to scold her further. He took the coffee in the battered old saucepan and drank. It tasted terrible, a mixture of rust and mould and instant coffee powder, but he wouldn't have dreamed of complaining.

'It was right, what you said about Joe Sugden going shooting,' he remarked as he set the saucepan down.

She looked puzzled. 'Don't know why you were interested,' she said. And then, struck by a thought, 'Steve, you didn't go to him for help? You didn't tell him?'

Steve shook his head. 'No, we mustn't tell anybody about us. If we do, they're sure to drag you home. And I'm not having that. Once for all, Pip, we got to get you away from that mother of yours and go out for what we want in life.'

She sighed. 'We can't do much without money, Steve.' She fell silent a moment then added, 'I wonder now if I was right to run off. I –'

'You're changing your mind? *You* don't want us to get wed?'

'Oh, I do, Steve, of course I do! But happen we should've waited a week or so before I left the house. I could have got a few things together –'

'Pip, you know we've been hesitating and talking for nigh on a month. Time's going by. We *got* to make a decision. And at least last night was a start. Next thing is to get to a city – Leeds or Manchester or somewhere ...'

'But that takes money, Steve.'

'We'll get money.'

'But how?'

'I dunno yet. But we'll get it.'

At Emmerdale, Joe had handed over his bag to his mother with the comment that he thought he might get a couple next day, quick and easy, if she thought the pair at the Woolpack would like them.

'Oh, I'm sure they would,' she said. 'Henry loves a good rabbit pie.'

'Make more sense to bake the pie and send it to them,' her father remarked. 'Otherwise Dolly will have to bake it for 'em.'

'Well, what's wrong with that?' Joe said, then added, 'Where is Dolly?'

'Helping Matt in t'mistle.'

'She's never learning to milk?'

'She is,' Annie said with a hidden smile.

'I'd best get in there afore she scares the herd to death,' Joe said, and shed his jacket. 'I'll finish up in there and then I'll be off down to Demdyke, Ma. I want to put t'gun away — never like to have it sitting about in the Landrover.'

'How was Pip?' Annie inquired.

'Oh ... Never turned up.'

'Oh?'

'In trouble with her Ma again, I s'pose. Honestly, from things she's told me, it's more like a reform school than a home, that place.'

Sighing, Joe went to join the others in the cowshed. Annie went back to her letter-writing on behalf of the Church Outing Committee.

'She's a nice little thing, is that Pip Coulter,' Sam remarked, watching her pen move over the paper. 'Hardly seems fair, she's saddled with a mother like that.'

Annie glanced up. 'I tried,' she confessed. 'I tried to talk to Pam. She shut the door in my face.'

'She what?'

'You know how she is, Dad. Edgy and quick to get on her high horse. She told me not to talk about her daughter.'

'Trouble with Pam Coulter,' Sam said, 'she's always been jealous of you.'

'What?' his daughter said, astounded.

'Always. Ever since she was a tot. 'Course, you being older, you were always ahead of her in everything. It's hardly likely she'd take advice from you ...'

'Dear me,' Annie sighed. 'I never suspected that.'

'How'd it be if I said a word to her?'

'To Pam Coulter? Dad, you've hardly ever exchanged a hello with her.'

'But I know Will, don't I? On the bowls team. I could happen drop a hint ...'

Annie knew her father's hints. 'Better not,' she said.

But Sam wasn't daunted. That evening after tea he made

it his business to be near the Coulters' home as Will drove home from his day's work.

'Hi, Will, did you do anything about a new bag for your woods?'

'Nay, Pam says I ought to be able to get t'old one mended.'

'That's just what I came to tell you. There's a great cobbler in Littlewell – can mend anything made wi' leather. That old bag o' yours is the genuine article, isn't it?'

'Certainly is. Was my Dad's, and his Dad's afore him.'

'Then Pinkey of Littlewell can mend it, I bet.' Sam hesitated. 'Mind if I come in and take a look? I like old things, tha knows.'

'I ... er ... well ...' stammered Will.

The door of his house flew open and Mrs Coulter appeared on the doorstep. 'Are you coming in, Will, or are you going to stand there gossiping all night?'

'Nay, lass I were just telling Sam ...'

'It were about his bowls, Mrs Coulter. Fine old woods, they deserve a fine old carrier –'

'Toys of the devil,' Pam Coulter said, casting up her eyes. 'No wonder we've been punished, when you insist on playing games of chance –'

'Bowls?' Sam cried, stricken. 'Bowls is a game of skill –'

'It's a waste of a Christian man's time, and God sees all, Sam Pearson. He sets His heavy hand on those who waste His time.'

'You been punished, then?' Sam said in a low voice to Will.

'Eh ... Sam,' breathed Will. 'Our Pip ...'

'What about her?' There was real alarm in Sam's tone, for Will looked almost desperate.

'Climbed out of her bedroom last night,' Will whispered, 'and not a word from her since!'

'Will!' shrilled his wife. 'Your tea's ready, and Mr Pangrave is coming at half-six to pray with us in this time of trial!'

With a hunted look at Sam, Will scuttled indoors.

Sam was astounded. Their daughter had run away, and instead of asking their friends and neighbours to help look for her, they were going to sit indoors being prayed over by a stranger!

Sam felt he might as well drop in at the Woolpack for a

glass of cider before heading for home to report this state of affairs to Annie. For some reason, Annie had got involved in Pip's welfare. He felt sure it was because the vicar had asked for her help, though how the vicar could be dragged into the affairs of chapel-goers, Sam didn't quite see.

In the Woolpack he found his grandson, teasing Amos about Dolly's new career as stockman. 'Stock person, I suppose you have to call her these days,' Joe was saying. 'But she's turning out a dab hand at it. You'll lose her soon, Amos. She'll be champion milking-hand and give demonstrations at the Yorkshire.'

'I would never stand in Miss Acaster's way if she wished to take up another career,' Amos said, 'though after all the trouble I've taken to teach her her craft as bar-person, I should think it strange.'

'Coo-er,' Joe said. 'That sounds like summat you wrote up for t'*Courier*.' He waved to Sam. 'Hello, Grandad. Usual?'

'Aye, thanks, Joe.' Sam found a seat. The place was half full, with plenty of cheerful chatter. He let the sounds run over him, pleased to be here but still a little perturbed at the thought of the trouble in the Coulter household. Poor little girl ... A pretty little thing, always bright and polite ...

'Here's your cider, Grandad. Anything wrong?'

'Nothing to get concerned about,' Sam said, thinking that it was a matter of confidence, not to be spread about. 'How did Henry take to your offer of fresh rabbit?'

'That were right grand,' Henry called from along the bar. 'Nothing like a good tasty rabbit pie. Dolly says she'll have a go tomorrow night, we can have it for tea. Not bad, eh?'

'If you don't mind picking lead shot out from every mouthful,' Amos said in gloom.

'Let me tell you, my good sir,' Joe rejoined, 'that's not my way of shooting. I don't pepper everything with shot. One good sight at the head and that's it.'

'That's a good old gun,' Henry said. 'Twelve bore, is it?'

'Aye. I like it. It settles nicely on your shoulder.'

'Got it with you?'

'You're joking,' Joe said. 'It's safe at home in the cupboard at Demdyke.'

It seemed to Sam that someone dropped something on the far side of the room, but when he turned his head all he saw was young Steve Hawker gathering up a broken ashtray. 'Sorry, Mr Brearley,' the lad said. 'It just sort of fell off the table.'

'If folks flail their arms about, then ashtrays are going to fall off tables,' Amos said in annoyance.

'I said I'm sorry.'

'Are you having anything else to drink?'

'I ... er ... nay, I'll take two tins of Coca Cola to take out and two packets of crisps.'

'Huh,' grunted Amos under his breath. Balanced against the cost of a new ashtray, Steve Hawker's custom was hardly worth having. All he'd had while in the pub was a half of mild, and he'd made that last as long as he could, almost as if he was waiting for someone.

Steve was in fact waiting. Waiting for Joe Sugden to show up, because then – he'd thought – the shotgun would be outside in the Landrover, easy to get at. Now he learned it was in a cupboard at Demdyke. Well, happen that was better.

Steve put the cans of soft drink and the crisps in the capacious pockets of his camouflage jacket, then hurried out. It was a short walk to Demdyke Row. He had no difficulty in getting into the house, for like most local inhabitants Joe left a key under the doormat. He walked in. The living room of the house was immediately inside the door, with a cupboard for coats. The gun wasn't there.

But that was too easy a place to leave a gun; Joe was more careful with firearms than that. After a moment's thought Steve went upstairs to the one bedroom that was furnished and opened the built-in cupboard.

There it was, still shielded in its sacking. The cartridges were in a separate, smaller sack. He picked up the gun, weighed it a moment in his hand like a Red Indian hefting his spear, then with sudden decision turned and hurried out.

It was quite difficult riding a bike with a shotgun tied to the frame. From time to time he almost giggled to himself at the comicality of his progress. But when he got the gun into the old cottage in the woods above the millstream, all his amusement vanished when he saw how Pip reacted.

'Steve,' she gasped in horror as he unwrapped it. 'Steve, where did you get that?'

'It's Joe Sugden's, isn't it?' he said, sharp with her, annoyed that she should be so shaken. 'What else did you think I was

32

after, chatting him up this afternoon?'

'But ... did he give it to you?'

'Course not. I took it.'

'Took it?'

'Look, we need money, don't we? And with this, we can get it.'

'But ... I don't understand. Steve, what do you mean? Get money ... with a gun?'

'Yeah, nobody argues with a gun, do they?'

'You mean ... you're going to *hold up* somebody?'

Steve was putting cartridges in the breach. 'Great, isn't it,' he said, meaning the clean precision of the mechanism.

'Great? Shooting somebody?'

'Oh, good grief, we're not going to shoot anybody!' he cried in annoyance. 'It's just to scare 'em. We'll just walk in, show the gun, and we'll get whatever we ask for.'

'No!'

'What d'you mean, no? We agreed, didn't we? We have to get to a big town so we can get married – no fuss, no inquiries. We can't do it in Beckindale like anybody else would. It's lucky for some,' he said, bitterly, 'they've got families they can discuss things with. But we haven't, so we've got to get money to keep us for a bit.'

'I don't ... There must be some way ... I can't take something from someone at gun point, Steve.'

'You don't have to do it,' he said. 'I'll do it. If you feel like that about it, I'll go on my own.'

'Oh, no –'

'But of course it's riskier, being on your own. I might get jumped –'

'Steve!'

'And then I'd be off to the pokey, and you'd be on your own, wouldn't you –'

'Steve! No, no, I'll go with you. Only ...'

'What?'

'Promise me you won't fire it. Promise me nobody will get hurt.'

'Course not. Don't be silly.'

'I just ... can't bear the thought, Steve.'

'No, everything will be all right. We'll just get the money and then we'll go, and it'll all be over. You and me together ... Nobody to spoil things. Eh?'

'Oh, yes, Steve. Once we get away from here ...'

'Everything will be different. We'll be together. We'll be Mr and Mrs Hawker. Won't that be great!'

She raised trusting, tear-filled eyes to him. 'Oh, it'll be so wonderful, Steve.'

His influence over her was so complete that she didn't even query it when he said he just must hurry back to his home to collect his gear and some tools. She waited quietly in the dark cottage until he returned, bringing candles and some old black polythene to make blinds at the window. He lit the candles and set to work with the tools. They proved to be a vice and a hacksaw. He began to saw the barrel of the gun.

'What's that for, Steve?'

'It's better. Less to show when you carry it.'

'Oh, yes, I see.'

'It won't take long. And then it'll be about the right time, and we'll get down there, and then we'll be off.'

'Yes ...' She sat watching him, sitting on the stone floor, arms around her knees, a frown of anxiety on her brow.

At last the four inches of barrel fell away. Steve blew the fragments of metal from the rim. 'There,' he said, and slipped the gun into the inner pocket of his jacket. The shortened gun fitted snugly below his armpit.

'Now, come on, time to get ready.'

'Steve, do we have to?'

'Of course we do. Come on – you can wear a pair of my jeans. Roll up the bottoms a bit – and you better have my spare jacket. You want to look like a boy, see. Only, don't speak. Let me do all the talking.'

As if hypnotised she obeyed. When they were ready, Steve shook his head. 'Forgot something, didn't we? Here.' He handed her a stocking mask.

A shudder of revulsion seized her. 'Oh no ... I can't, I can't!'

He took her by the shoulders and shook her. 'I'm going on my own if you won't come,' he warned. 'And whether I get back here to collect you is a big question. I may just have to keep on going.'

'No, Steve! Don't leave me!'

'Come on then.' He urged her out, his arm around her. From that moment on, he never allowed her time to draw breath enough to make a further protest.

34

As they came into the outskirts of Beckindale it was about eleven-thirty. 'It's going to be a piece of cake,' Steve whispered. 'Just you do as I tell you, don't say a word, and everything will be easy. Right?'

She shivered and nodded. Steve led the way along the deserted lane that brought them to the back of the Woolpack. Though the bar was in darkness, light was showing from the backroom. Steve knocked on the door with the stock of the shotgun.

Muffled sounds came from within – Amos's voice raised in query, footsteps, and the lock turning.

'We're closed,' Amos said in a voice of annoyance.

'Not now, you're not,' Steve said, stepping forward and pushing the gun under Amos's chin. 'Let's go inside.'

'Hey – what –'

'Not a word,' Steve warned.

Henry Wilks was by the fridge looking for milk for his cocoa. He turned. His eyes went wide.

'Not a word or he gets it,' hissed Steve.

'Now look here –' Amos began.

The gun was jerked under his chin so ferociously that the words were cut off.

'Don't do owt,' Henry gasped, 'let 'em have what they want.'

'That's the ticket,' Steve said. 'And for a start, put your hands up.'

There was a moment's incredulous silence. And then Amos Brearley and Henry Wilks put their hands above their heads.

CHAPTER THREE

Every licensee has at some time thought about being robbed. The notion had been brought to the forefront of Henry's mind a few weeks ago, when the Butterworth Ball went missing. But that had so plainly been the work of a hoaxer that there had been no sense of alarm, and Henry had laughed Amos out of the precautions he then began.

How bitterly he regretted that now, as they gazed down the barrel of the shotgun.

'Now, where's the money?' asked the hold-up man.

Amos looked beseechingly at Henry. He was saying, 'Don't tell him.' But for Henry discretion was the greater part of valour. He nodded at the bag containing the evening's takings, which was sitting on the table.

The robber picked up the bag and hefted it. It was impossible to tell whether he was pleased or disappointed, for his face was distorted by its stocking mask.

'You,' he said, 'take your coat off.'

Henry obediently took off his jacket.

'Chuck it on the table.'

Henry did so. The gunman jerked his head at his accomplice, to come forward and pick up the jacket. 'Where are the keys?' he demanded, looking at Amos.

'I don't know,' Amos lied.

Oh, Amos! thought Henry. This was no time to be stubborn. 'There's some in my pocket,' he said, 'and the rest on the hook inside the back door.'

'Get them,' the gunman said to his helper. The lad went quickly to the hook and lifted the keys. 'Which is the cellar door?' the gunman went on.

'That one.' Henry nodded at the door immediately inside the living quarters.

'Open it.'

'Can't,' Amos blurted. 'It's locked.'

36

'Which key?'

Amos looked mutinous.

'You, show us,' the gunman said with a jerk of the shot-gun at Henry.

Feeling like Burgess and Maclean rolled into one for his treachery, Henry showed him which key opened the cellar door. 'Right, you unlock,' he was told. Henry did so.

'Get in there – go on.'

They went down the cellar steps. It was pitch dark, and some instinct told Henry that Amos was scheming some wild plan of attack. Quickly he found the switch and put on the light. Amos was momentarily outlined with a hand reaching out for one of the coopering tools hanging on the stair-case wall. He dropped his hand. The gunman either didn't see or chose not to remark on it.

Henry went down behind Amos. When they were both about six steps below the livingroom level, the door slammed shut on them and the key turned in the lock.

'Oh, heck!' groaned Amos, 'he's locked us in!'

'That's what I thought he was going to do,' Henry said.

'Mr Wilks, if you hadn't been so quick to switch on the light, I were going to disarm him with a spokeshave.'

'Amos, that was me right behind you. I didn't fancy getting brained.'

'Shh,' hissed Amos. They stood on the stairs and listened. They heard the click of the room light going off, the slam of the back door. 'They've gone,' Amos said. 'Come on.'

He rushed up the stairs to the door. Henry stood back to let him pass. Amos seized the handle, turned it this way and that, then slumped against the door.

'It's locked!'

'But you knew that, Amos.'

'I just thought ... happen the lock didn't take. It some-times doesn't.'

'You could be sure that lad made sure the lock took. He knew what he were about, that one.'

Amos sat down on the nearest step and put his head in his hands.

'You all right, Amos?' Henry said in alarm.

'No, I'm not, Mr Wilks. If you want to know, I'm ... I'm humiliated! Right humiliated. Having to give in to a couple o' young louts like that!'

'They had the gun, Amos. You can't argue with a gun.'

37

'I *know* that, Mr Wilks. I'm ex-Artillery.' He sprang up. 'I'd like to get my hands on 'em.'

'Me too,' admitted Henry. He hadn't enjoyed playing a Weak Willie to those two. But he had always remembered, as he obeyed the gunman's orders, Joe's remarks about rabbit-shooting. 'One good sight at the head and that's it.' And the young man holding the sawn-off shotgun had that scary look about him, keyed up and nervy ...

'Can we get out?' he asked Amos.

'Not without t'key – or a battering ram,' was the morose reply.

'Eh, Amos ... this is a well-built old place, isn't it! Not a chance of pushing the door down.'

'Not a chance.'

'What about the delivery trap?'

They went down the cellar steps to the centre of the vault and stared up into the ceiling. The light wasn't really good enough to be able to see much, but if the light had been the other way about – if it had been daylight outside and dimness in the cellar – they'd have been able to see edges of brightness round the delivery trapdoor, which was set into the paving just outside the Woolpack.

'I suppose it's padlocked?' Henry said despondently.

'Certainly. You know I always padlock it the minute the deliveryman's gone.'

'Aye,' said Henry. Curses on the efficiency of his finicky partner. 'Well, shall we try a yell?'

'Nobody'll hear us this time o'night.'

Henry sighed. 'Suggest something else, then.'

Amos pondered. 'Nay,' he said, 'I can't think of a thing.'

'Right. Both together, after three. One ... two ... three!'

'He-elp!'

But at ten minutes to twelve in Beckindale, who would be about to hear subterranean voices calling for help?

Joe Sugden was, in fact, about. But not near enough the Woolpack to hear the cries. He had gone on to Hotten to a disco after a drink or so at the Woolpack, and got home about a quarter to twelve. Tired and ready to fall into bed, he'd gone indoors without switching on any lights, and walked upstairs.

With the result that he'd walked into a cupboard door in the bedroom, giving himself a painful bang on the forehead.

38

When he'd put on the light he found the cupboard door open, knew he'd left it shut, and with one quick look inside learned the worst. His twelve-bore was gone.

He hurried out of Demdyke and went to the public phone box. He dialled 999. When he'd been put through to the police, he found himself talking to Ted Lessiter, the local sergeant. 'Hello, Ted, this is Joe Sugden ... Aye, but I'm not at Emmerdale ... No, public box. Listen, my shotgun's been stolen from my house.'

'You what?' Ted said in dismay. Joe Sugden was the last man he'd have thought of as being careless with guns. 'Where was it?'

'Cupboard in an upstairs bedroom. No, nothing else's been taken, so far as I could see – didn't wait to do an inventory, though. Just when I saw the gun was gone ... Yeh, and cartridges.'

'Damn,' groaned Ted. It always meant trouble, gun thefts.

When Ted had told him to touch nothing and wait for him, Joe put through a call to Emmerdale. It was unlikely there would be an intruder there, but you never could tell. Matt answered, on his way to bed as the phone rang.

'Matt, Demdyke's been broken into and my gun's gone. I thought I'd just –'

'Broken into? Door busted, or window forced, you mean?'

'Nay,' said Joe, 'now you mention it ... Hell, he probably used the spare key.'

'Under the mat, was it?'

'Aye.'

'Have you told the police?'

'Aye, Ted Lessiter's on his way.'

'I hate to think what he's going to say when he hears you leave a key under the mat.'

'But everybody does that.'

'Aye, I suppose so.'

'I just thought I'd warn you to lock up proper tonight, eh?'

'Righto.'

'See you in the morning.'

'Aye.'

The sergeant drove up as Joe finished a thorough looking-over at Demdyke. 'Anything other than the gun?' he asked.

'Nope.'

'How d'he get in?'

39

Joe went red. 'Key under the mat. It's gone.'

'Oh, Joe.'

'I know, don't tell me.'

'And you had a gun in an unlocked cupboard indoors?'

'But I never imagined ...'

'How many folk knew you had it?'

'Well ... anybody, I suppose. It weren't a secret.'

Lessiter sighed. 'Well, let's hope it's just some silly kid wanting to take pot shots at pigeons. Worrisome, when a gun's taken. It generally means it's needed for something naughty.'

'I'm sorry, Ted.'

'I know you are. You'll be more careful next time, eh?'

'Won't I just.'

'Well, let's hope we don't hear of it in a hold-up.'

'That's right, rub it in.'

If Sergeant Lessiter had gone for a walk around Beckindale then, he might well have heard of the gun having been used in a hold-up. He at least would have heard Amos and Henry, calling desperately up towards the delivery trap of the cellar. But Sergeant Lessiter drove back to Hotten, to put in a report so that it could go out to patrol cars and put the patrols on the alert for any armed crime later that night.

The criminals who had held up the Woolpack were examining their spoils in the ruined cottage above the millrace. 'Not bad,' Steve said, counting the notes he had added to the cash in the leather bag. 'What with the takings and the money in the wallet, there's close on ninety pounds.'

Pip was staring fixedly at the tiny fire in the dilapidated grate.

'Soon as it's light we'll get across to Hotten,' Steve went on. 'There's a train to Leeds at half-six. Once there, we're laughing.'

He looked at her eagerly. She made no reply.

'What's the matter?'

'Where are we going to live?'

'We'll find somewhere, like we agreed.'

'We haven't agreed about *how* we're going to live.'

He hesitated. He knew what she meant. So far their plans had gone no further than getting her away from her terrible home, to some place where they could be free and happy.

Now they had taken the first step – the first terrible step – and she was afraid. It was in her eyes. She felt that happiness based on wickedness couldn't prosper.

'I'll get a job,' he began. 'There'll be something –'

'Will it be so easy, Steve? I keep hearing on the news bulletins. About unemployment ...'

'I'll find something.'

'Only, I've been thinking. I mean ... we did it once, took what wasn't ours ...'

'We won't do it again. I swear.'

'Steve ... could we give back the money? Now, before we're branded as criminals?'

'How'd we get to Leeds, then?'

'Well, take some, take enough. Return the rest.'

'Little or a lot, we'd have stolen it.'

'But give an I.O.U. to say we'd repay ...'

'Pip,' he said, almost in despair, 'it's done. Don't you understand? We did it. We held them up with a gun. You can't cancel it out. All we can do is go forward now.'

'I just can't see what we can look forward to, Steve.'

'We'll be together. That's better, any road, than what we're leaving.'

He held her close, and after a moment she nodded her head against his chest and said, 'Yes.' He knew he had won; they would go to Leeds as soon as it was light.

In the cellar at the Woolpack, the night was progressing by slow degrees. Amos and Henry had yelled themselves hoarse for the time being.

'I'll tell thee summat,' Henry observed, hugging his shirt-sleeved arms against himself, 'it's none too warm down here.'

Amos gave him a glare. 'Mr Wilks, you don't keep good beer in a warm cellar.'

'I know that, Amos, I were only saying it's chilly. I've no jacket, sitha.'

'If you hadn't taken it off when that yobbo told you to, you wouldn't be cold.'

'Amos, he was after my wallet and things. I'd rather he got it off me by taking my jacket.'

'Huh,' Amos said. 'He were only thin and young. We could've handled him. As for the other – that was nobbut a babby.'

'A female babby,' Henry observed.

'What?'

'A girl, Amos.'

'What was?'

'The other robber. That was a girl.'

'A girl?'

'Aye.'

'Are you saying we were held up by a lad and a lass?'

'Aye.'

Amos said nothing for a long moment during which his face went from white to red, from red to puce, and from puce to a greenish hue.

'If I thought that were true,' he said, 'I'd shoot meself.'

'It's true, Amos. The one who didn't speak was a girl.'

'That canna be true.'

'It's true.'

'But ... but ... I mean, how would you know?'

Henry smothered a smile. 'For one thing, she was wearing scent.'

Amos hesitated, tugged at his side whiskers, then blurted, 'After shave!'

'Lads of that type don't wear after shave. I tell you it was scent. At least, it was something wi' scent in it – hand lotion, happen.'

'But fellers use hand lotion sometimes.'

'But that wasn't a feller.'

'You can't be sure.'

'I'm sure, Amos.'

'But how can you be sure?'

Henry sighed. Should he begin instruction on the birds and the bees? The fact was, the curves of the girl's body, slender though they were, couldn't be hidden by the rough clothes she wore. After a moment's hesitation Henry said, 'Did you see her feet?'

'I ... er ... no, I don't believe I did.'

'She had the bottoms of her jeans rolled up. They were far too long. And her feet were in little bitty shoes. Flat heeled, mind, but girl's shoes. About size three and a half, I'd say.'

'Oh,' said Amos, convinced. 'Oh ...' Then, groaning, '*Oh!* The humiliation! To be robbed by a bit of a girl!'

'And a lad wi' a shotgun.'

'Aye, that makes it more bearable. But I'll never hold up my head again.'

'What's the time?' asked Henry.

'Two o'clock.'

'Is it time to give another shout?'

'Nobody's going to hear us at two a.m.'

'In that case,' Henry said, gazing about, 'I think I'll have a glass of scotch to warm me up.'

'Mr Wilks!'

'Now what's the matter?'

'You're not going to take to drink?'

'As a matter of fact, I think I am. Here we are, locked in a cellar with drink all around us and nothing else to do. If a man could ever be excused for getting roaring drunk, now's the time.'

'But ... it's so much against my calling ... to break into my own stocks and get drunk!'

'All right then, Amos. We won't get drunk. But I really feel justified in opening a bottle of scotch and getting some comfort from that.'

'I forbid you,' Amos said. Then, as Henry raised his brows, 'At least, I strongly disagree. You never know where it might end, Mr Wilks. And the scotch down here is the best in the house.'

'So that's it! You wouldn't mind me getting drunk on the run-of-the-mill brands, but you don't want to see me swigging Glen Livet?'

Amos looked helpless. Then, since he could think of nothing better to do, he sprang up, took his position under the trap, and roared, 'Help! Anybody! He-elp!'

No help came. Henry opened a bottle of scotch. There was no glass and he had to drink from the bottle. Amos was scandalised. But by the time four o'clock came, even Amos had given in sufficiently to drink a few mouthfuls of whisky from the bottle and settle down to sleep in chilly restlessness.

Soon after that hour, in the cottage in the woods, Pip and Steve were packing to leave for the train. A cold, steely morning had begun to show light in the sky. Shivering with apprehension and exhaustion, Pip followed Steve out of the cottage.

The way through the woods was frightening in the half-light. She stumbled and fell more than once. When they reached the muddy path down to the brook, she could scarcely keep her footing at all. He had to hold her by the arm. They came out by the road, and he wanted to cross the upper slopes and take a detour to get to Hotten. But already he was doubtful if she could make it in time for the train.

The only thing to do was take the short cut, across Emmerdale's fields to the main road. It would be all right. No one was about yet.

On the main road, a patrol car was moving quietly, the policeman at the wheel on the alert. Sergeant Lessiter had said to keep an eye out for anyone of the troublesome kind, but had addressed the message to cars on the outskirts of the towns. However, P.C. Edwards felt that the thief who'd taken the shotgun might not have got far yet. So he was keeping lookout nearer to Beckindale.

He saw the two figures in the mist rising from the Emmerdale ley fields furthest from the farm. Two young lads, it looked like. Odd. There were no boys that young in the Sugden family.

Best to take a look. He eased the car to a standstill and got out. 'Hi!' he shouted.

The two figures stopped short, froze, then leapt into life. 'Hi!' shouted Edwards again, scrambling over the dyke. But they were off, across the field, the taller of the two dragging the little feller by the arm.

They ran down the slope into the cover of some hazels. Then as he approached they rushed out, veering, and heading for easier ground. They came out on the track to the field gate which stood open because Joe had intended to bring machinery in during the day.

Steve didn't know the area of the farm very well. He found to his dismay that he'd run them straight into the farmyard.

He could hear the constable pounding after them. A figure came out of a shed across the yard – Joe Sugden, about to start milking.

Joe heard Edwards shouting. 'What's that?' he said, to no one in particular.

Matt came behind him to the door of the mistle. 'Summat's up,' he murmured. They came out together into the yard, staring out towards the lane.

Joe's grandfather, up early to find a piece of wood-carving he'd started weeks ago and intended to finish today, heard the sounds from his toolshed on the other side of the yard. He looked out of the window but there was nothing to be

44

seen from that angle. But the sound of running footsteps was quite clear now. He came out on to the top of the flight of steps that led up to his shed.

'What's afoot?' he asked.

'Dunno, Grandad. Folks out on the lane –'

At that moment Steve Hawker came careering into the farmyard, Pip at his elbow. From behind came the voice of Constable Edwards. 'Stop them!'

Joe stepped in front of them. 'Hey Steve – what – ?'

At once Steve jinked to one side, dragged Pip by the wrist, and was at the foot of the steps leading to the toolshed. At the top, Sam Pearson gaped at them with amazement. 'What's to do here?' he demanded.

Steve had no breath for a reply. He pulled Pip up the stairs, shoved Sam back into the shed, and made as if to follow.

'Now wait a minute, lad –'

All at once Steve's other hand came up, the one not holding Pip. It held the shotgun. 'Get inside,' he gasped.

'Now look here –'

But the sheer momentum of Steve's movement almost overbalanced the old man. He went back on his heels, into his shed.

At that moment Joe and Matt reached the foot of the steps. 'Steve!' Joe shouted. 'What the hell are you up to?' He was on his way up when Constable Edwards grabbed him from behind.

'He's got a gun,' he panted.

'I could see that,' Joe snorted, trying to pull free, 'but that's my grandad!'

'Keep back,' Edwards said, in the voice of authority that cannot be gainsaid. 'We don't want murder done here.'

'What?' Joe gasped.

'Hey-up, Joe,' Matt said, dragging him down to ground level. 'He's right. That lad's in a right state.'

'He wouldn't hurt Grandad?'

'I wouldn't take a bet on it,' the constable said. He urged them away from the foot of the steps, to the corner of the building. He jerked his head upwards. 'Is there any way out of there other than them steps?'

'Nay. That's Grandad's workshop.'

'Then we've got 'em.'

45

'And they've got Grandad!' cried Matt.

'Aye,' said the constable in a heavy tone. 'Two damn silly young fools wi' a shotgun ... wi' an old man at t'other end of barrel.' He saw the other two men stare at him with disbelief. 'It's happening,' he assured them. 'You on the phone here?'

'Aye ... In t'house.'

'Show me.'

Matt led the way. Joe stubbornly remained where he was. 'Come on,' said the constable.

'I'm not budging from here.'

The constable hesitated. Then he said, 'All right. But don't thee do nowt. Nowt, understand?'

'But what about Grandad?'

'That's why you're to do nowt. They've already shot at me.'

'Shot at you? Steve shot at you?'

'Aye, as we turned into the lane.'

Joe shook his head. 'It must have gone off accidentally,' he said. 'Steve Hawker never would do a thing like that.'

As if on cue, the window of the workshop creaked open. 'Keep off,' shouted Steve Hawker, 'or t'old feller gets it through the head!'

CHAPTER FOUR

The door of the farmhouse was already open as Constable Edwards reached it. Annie Sugden was framed in the opening. 'What's going on out there?' she asked in alarm.

'Er ... Mrs Sugden, isn't it?' Edwards said, suddenly getting his bearings and realising where he was. 'Can I use your phone?'

'Of course. Come in.' She stood aside, to reveal Dolly Acaster in a dressing-gown. Dolly grasped Annie arm, so that Annie could hardly get out of the policeman's way as he hurried in. 'Trouble, is it?' she asked.

'Some young lout with a shotgun,' Edwards said over his shoulder. 'Holed up in one of your outbuildings –'

'Matt!' cried Dolly, about to rush out.

'Nay, don't go out there,' the constable said. 'Matt ... That's the fair lad, isn't it? He's all right. He's round t'corner of the workshop with the other one – that's Joe, isn't it?'

'Yes. He's all right?'

'Right as rain, so far,' Edwards said, dialling. 'Joe Sugden ... ? Ha. Now we know where his shotgun got to.'

'Oh, but that's –'

'Police,' the constable said into the phone, and then to Annie, 'If you don't mind, Mrs Sugden, I've got to attend to this. We need help in a hostage situation.'

'Hostage?' Annie gasped.

'He's got an old gentleman ...' The phone quacked, and Edwards began to speak into it earnestly.

'Dad!' said Annie, and made as if to go out.

'No, Mrs Sugden,' Dolly protested, catching at her. 'Don't. Wait till we hear what the situation is.'

They stood in tense silence while the constable reported back to headquarters and was given instructions. When he replaced the receiver they were quick to speak. 'Is my father

47

all right? Who is it up there with him? What's he doing it for?'

'Damned if I know,' Edwards said, answering the last question first. 'I was told to keep an eye out for suspicious characters with a gun. I saw these two over the rise and called –'

'Two of them?'

'Aye, one's younger than the other, I reckon – being led on. Any road, all I did was shout to ask who they were, and they were off. Next thing I knew, when I got out of the car to follow 'em, a spray of shot went past my ear.'

'He shot at you?'

'He did that.' Edwards strode to the door. 'Best get back out there and see what he's up to. Nothing much, I reckon, or your Joe would've given a shout.'

Out in the yard, he glimpsed Joe and Matt round the corner of the workshop. Joe signalled to him to wait, and went round the far side of the workshop, to come by a roundabout route through the milking parlour and out alongside the policeman.

'That's Steve Hawker up there,' he said.

'Steve Hawker? Who's he? Anybody?'

'Nobody at all. I don't know what's got into him. But I can guess how he got that gun.'

'Yeah,' said Edwards, frowning at Joe.

'Well, I've said I'm sorry if I was careless,' Joe muttered. 'But it never crossed my mind he was asking questions about it with that in mind.'

'What in mind, exactly?' Edwards said. 'Has he said anything?'

'Only "Keep off" and daft things about shooting Grandad.'

'Happen it's not so daft. He took a shot at me.'

'I dunno,' Joe said helplessly. 'He's always seemed a quiet enough feller. A bit of a chancer, but no harm in him.'

'Must have had something in mind to steal the gun in the first place.'

'But not this, surely? Holding up my Grandad? Grandad never did anybody any harm in his life.'

'Hi!' came a voice from the workshop. 'Hi, you there! You ready to hear my terms?'

'Hear his terms,' echoed Edwards, going red with anger.

48

'Cheeky young tyke! I'll tan his hide when I get hold of him.'

They could hear a police car approaching on the road. 'Better hear what he wants,' Edwards said. 'Then I'll have the news for the sergeant.'

He went into the centre of the farmyard so that he could be clearly seen from the window of the workshop. 'What d'you want?' he called.

'Right! I'm only going to say this once. I want a car brought to the foot of the steps, and everybody to stand away, and a clear road from here to the motorway. Or else.'

'Or else what?' called Edwards, annoyed at the silly gangsterism.

'Or else Mr Pearson gets it.'

'No go, lad. Throw out the gun and come down.'

'You must be joking! A car with petrol, and keys in the ignition. I got the gun trained on the old feller.'

'You're wasting your time, Steve. We never make deals with kidnappers.'

'Who said anything about kidnapping? *I* don't want the old chap. All I want is for me and my mate to get out of here. So that's the terms – a car and a clear road.'

'Now listen, boy, be sensible –'

'No more talk. That's final.'

'Steve – !'

But there was no reply.

The constable hurried out to the gate where he could see the uniforms of the men from the newly arrived car. Sergeant Lessiter was there. 'Anything?'

'His terms are he wants a car and petrol, to get to the motorway.'

'That's not on.'

'I told him so.'

'Has he harmed the old man?'

'No idea. Can't see him.'

'Go back and ask to speak to Mr Pearson.'

Events had placed Constable Edwards in the position of go-between. He went back to the farmyard and called: 'Steve. Steven Hawker!'

'Got that car ready?'

'First we want to know that Mr Pearson's all right.'

'He's all right.'

'Let me hear him say that for himself.'

'You can take my word.'

'No fear. I want to hear Mr Pearson himself.'

Sam, inside the workshop in which he'd spent many a busy hour, heard the conversation with interest. It all seemed to be happening to someone else. When Steve, in exasperation, turned to him and motioned him to come to the window, he almost didn't obey – he couldn't imagine he was being asked to play a part in this drama.

'Hello?' he called.

'That you, Mr Pearson?'

'Aye, it's me.'

Edwards looked at Joe, who nodded vigorously.

'Are you all right, Mr Pearson?'

'Aye, I'm fine. So's the lass.'

'The what?'

'Shurrup, you!' snarled Steve, shoving him away from the window.

'The lass?' exclaimed the constable to Joe. 'What lass?'

'God knows. I thought you said there was a lad with him?'

'I thought it was. A young 'un. Now I come to think on it ...' Edwards nodded to himself. 'It's a girl. Of course. Question is, is she there because she wants to be or has he brought her here at gunpoint?'

Joe threw out his hands. 'I can't understand a thing,' he said. 'Steve Hawker would never kidnap a lass, or pull a gun on an old man.'

'But he has, Joe.'

'Nay ... It's some sort of mistake.'

Matt was coming round from the outer side of the buildings to join them. 'What's on?' he asked.

'I was to find out if Mr Pearson was all right. I'd best report back. Mr Pearson says there's a girl there too.'

'Ha,' muttered Matt. 'I thought I recognised her as they ran by. Yon's Pip Coulter.'

'*What?*'

'Pip Coulter.'

'Talk sense, Matt.'

'I tell you, Joe, I thought so when they turned up. But we were all so had-up when he waved the gun at us I sort of forgot it. But he's got Pip Coulter up there.'

50

'I'll tell Sergeant Lessiter,' Edwards said, and hurried out.

The cows in the mistle were beginning to clamour for attention. Joe and Matt exchanged glances – troubled yet resigned. 'Whatever happens,' Joe said, with a bitter wryness, 'cows have got to be milked ...'

They went into the mistle. There was nothing more useful they could do for the moment.

In the kitchen Annie was making tea. Dolly had been upstairs to dress and now joined her. 'Any news?'

Annie shook her head. 'I heard them calling out to each other. I couldn't make out what they were saying.'

'Where's Matt?'

Annie gave her a sharp glance. 'Where do you think?' she asked. 'He's in the cow-shed, starting the milking machine.'

'At a time like this?' Dolly cried.

Annie's eyes softened. 'Ah, lass,' she said, her tone gentle, 'you'll have to come to terms with it. If the heavens fell, the milking's got to be done –'

'But a thing like this is more important than routine –'

'Think about it, Dolly. Cows suffer if they aren't milked. It's *got* to be done.'

'Oh.' Dolly was silent for a moment. 'Of course. I'm sorry.'

'Nowt to be sorry for. Tea?'

They were drinking theirs when the door opened and Constable Edwards came in. 'Mrs Sugden, can Sergeant Lessiter use your parlour as a control room?'

Annie raised her eyebrows. 'He's welcome to use the parlour,' she said. 'Control room ... whatever next? 'Is my father all right?'

'He spoke to me. Said he was okay. He told us there's a girl with the chap, and Matt says he thinks it's a girl called Pip Coulter.'

'Oh!' Annie gasped.

'What's wrong? That mean something to you?'

'She's been missing from her home for two nights now,' Annie explained. 'Will Coulter blurted it out to my father yesterday, that she'd climbed out her bedroom window.'

'You're sure she didn't return home?'

'Nay, I'm sure, for yesterday late evening Mrs Coulter was at t'vicarage accusing Vicar of harbouring her daughter –

51

and Pip wasn't at t'vicarage at all. That means they didn't know where she was.'

'But we know,' Edwards said slowly. 'She was with Steve Hawker.'

'Aye.'

'But against her will? Do we know that?'

Annie thought about it. She looked at Dolly, who sometimes gleaned information through her work at the Woolpack. But Dolly shook her head.

'Constable, Will Coulter said she'd climbed out of her bedroom. That sounds to me as if she went of her own accord – at least up to that point. I mean, Steve didn't order her out at gunpoint.'

'No, Mrs Sugden, that's right,' Dolly agreed. 'Pip went night before last, you say. Joe's gun was stolen *last* night.'

'Gets worse by the minute,' Edwards said. 'Can I tell the sergeant he can come in and bring a two-way radio?'

'Of course.'

In the toolshed Pip was sitting in dejection on the workbench, avoiding Sam's eye. Sam was perched uncomfortably on an old kitchen chair he'd brought here to mend many weeks ago.

'Lass, hast'a thought how thy father will take this?' he said to Pip.

'Shurrup!' growled Steve.

'And thine,' Sam said to him. 'Though mind, he's never been one to be too worried about right and wrong. But he won't thank thee for putting him in the forefront of a row like this.'

'I said shurrup!'

'But I allus liked Will Coulter,' Sam went on as if to himself. 'A kindly man ...'

'I don't want to hear about it,' Steve said. 'I told you, keep quiet.'

'You're never going to get away with it, tha knows,' Sam remarked.

'Oh yes I am! You heard them – wanted to make sure you were okay before they gave us the car.'

'They're never going to give you a car, lad.'

'No, that's right, Steve,' Pip quavered. 'They won't. You did one of the worst things – you shot at a policeman. They won't let you get off.'

'I never shot at him,' Steve cried.

'But I heard –'

'I shot in the air! To scare him off.'

'But they're never going to believe that, are they?'

'And who's to blame 'em?' Sam put in.

'I don't want to hear any more from you,' Steve ground out, thrusting the gun at Sam.

Sam flinched, but refused to allow any fear to show. 'What you going to do, shoot me?' he asked. 'Do that, and your goose is cooked, Steve.'

'He's right, Steve – stop waving the gun about ...'

'Don't you start getting at me too!'

'I only want to stop you from –'

'You're in this as well as me,' Steve insisted, anger flaring in the words. 'Don't forget that!'

'But I never meant to –'

'But you did, didn't you? Just the same as I did.'

She hung her head. 'Oh, what's it matter,' she whispered. 'We've got ourselves into the worst sort of trouble. Shooting at a policeman ...'

'I'll never believe it of Pip Coulter,' Annie was saying to Sergeant Lessiter, who was settling himself at the parlour table with a radio set. 'Nor Steve Hawker, neither. He's got faults, poor lad. But using a gun – never!'

'But it's a fact, Mrs Sugden. He shot at the constable.'

'Not deliberately.'

'Edwards hailed him and was greeted with a gunshot.'

'But why did he hail them? Did he suspect them of something?'

'Nay, not exactly. He was just checking.'

'I mean, was Steve running from the scene of a crime?'

Lessiter shook his head. 'No crime's been reported. That's what makes the whole thing so crazy.'

'There you are, then,' Annie said.

'Where am I, Mrs Sugden?'

'The lad was careless and pulled the trigger. Now he's scared and thinks he's for the high jump.'

'He is, too,' Lessiter said grimly, and gave his attention to the r-t set.

Annie went back to the kitchen, where Dolly was making nervy preparations for breakfast. Dolly wouldn't be easy in her mind until Matt and Joe had finished in the milking

53

parlour and come safely indoors.

The phone rang. Annie picked it up. 'Put me through to Sergeant Lessiter, please,' said a voice.

'He's on a radio thing in the parlour,' Annie said.

'Oh, in that case, call Constable Edwards to the phone, will you?'

'Just a moment.'

She went to the kitchen door, called to the constable, and saw him indoors. 'They asked for the sergeant first but as he's busy they want you.'

'Aye, communication links,' he commented, and went to the phone.

Annie cast a glance back at Dolly, who was putting bacon into the grill pan. Without a word she slipped out, taking her coat from the hook as she went.

Pip was keeping watch at the toolshed window now. 'Mrs Sugden's going somewhere,' she reported.

In a flash Steve was at her side, but all he saw was Annie Sugden with her coat slung over her shoulders, heading towards the barns.

'What's she going up there for?' he asked aloud.

'Calves to feed, or something?' suggested Pip.

Sam, after a momentary frown, made his face bland and expressionless.

'I don't like doing this to her,' Pip said in a quavering voice. 'She's always been nice to me.'

'We ain't doing anything to her.'

'He's her father,' she pointed out.

'That her bad luck. We just had to take what we had. He'll be all right so long as nobody tries anything funny.'

'Steve ... You wouldn't really ...?'

Steve met her tear-filled eyes, and his unformed, young face trembled as if he himself were near to tears. But he stiffened his lips and said with grimness, 'I got to take care of you. That's the important thing.'

'Not this way, Steve!'

'What other way have we got?'

A sound outside made him whip round to the window. He could see Annie's respectable saloon car nosing round from the barn into the farmyard.

'What's she up to?' yelled Steve, beside himself with terror.

Annie stepped out of the car, but on the side away from

the farmhouse. Steve pointed the gun down at her out of the window. She was within yards of the steps leading up to the workshop.

'Don't you come any nearer,' he warned.

She was gazing up at him. 'Sergeant Lessiter said you wanted a car,' she said. 'You can have this one – for the gun.'

Steve gave a gasp. Then he said, 'Oh yeah! And the cops waiting round the corner.'

'There's no one here but me. The sergeant's in my parlour tuning in a radio thing. Constable Edwards is on the phone in the kitchen. The two men who came with the sergeant are round the front of the house to make sure you don't get away that way. There are more men on their way from Hotten so if you want to go, now's your chance – you can drive out through the back gate, the farm gate, and be on the road to Connelton in five minutes.'

'Let's take it, Steve,' Pip urged, taking his elbow.

'Nay, it's a trap –'

'You'll get ten minutes start, happen, before the other police arrive.'

'Come on, Steve –'

'They put her up to it –'

'She wouldn't trick us, Steve. Not Mrs Sugden.'

'What are you up to?' Steve snarled, looking at Annie with a mixture of fear and longing.

'I'm trying to save my father and to prevent you doing any further damage,' Annie responded. 'So far you've killed nobody wi' that gun, Steve. Give it to me and take your chance with the car.'

'Please, Steve,' begged Pip.

'The longer you leave it the less chance you've got,' Annie warned.

Steve's nerve broke. 'All right,' he said, 'Come on!'

Pip fell upon the door and dragged it open. They came down the steps in a rush. 'Gi'e us the keys, then,' he demanded.

Annie held out her hand, closed and just beyond his reach. 'Throw away the gun first.'

Steve hesitated. Pip clutched pleadingly at his arm. With a snort of exasperation he threw the shotgun over the steps. Even as it hit the ground, Annie was handing over the car keys.

'Come on!' Steve panted. They fell into the car. As he

fumbled with the ignition Pip leaned out of the window. 'Thank you, Mrs Sugden.'

'Be careful, lass,' Annie said in a sad, gentle voice.

In a roar Steve got the engine going. He made a racing start out of the farmyard. The door of the farmhouse banged open to reveal Sergeant Lessiter and the constable. They tumbled out into the yard together, their faces incredulous as the car raced off.

'Is that them?' Lessiter yelled at Annie.

'Aye. And here's the gun.' She picked it up from the ground to hold it out by the barrel towards Lessiter.

'How the hell did that happen?'

'Are you all right, Dad?' Annie said, hurrying up the steps to the workshop.

Sam raised himself stiffly from the lopsided chair. 'Aye, lass,' he said, groaning, 'but I could do wi' my breakfast.'

She put her arm about him and almost hugged him. He allowed the embrace for a moment and then straightened. 'Tha shouldn't have done that, lass,' he reproved her. 'Bargaining with criminals ...'

'You'd rather have sat here in the cold without your breakfast, would you?'

Sergeant Lessiter came running in. 'You all right, sir?'

'I'm fine, or nearly so. Oh, it's young Tom Lessiter, isn't it?'

'That's right, Mr Pearson. That was a nasty experience. How the hell did they get that car, though?'

'Sergeant Lessiter, now you mind your language,' reproved Sam.

'Sorry, Mr Pearson. But we've slipped up here. We should have kept them boxed up –'

'And driven the lad to desperation,' Annie said. 'You said yourself he hadn't done anything wrong until Constable Edwards challenged him –'

'And then, s'far as I could make out from the things they said,' Sam put in, 'he fired in the air to put Edwards off.'

'That's *his* story. Where did that car come from?' Lessiter said.

'It's kept in the barn.'

'Oh, confound it. How did it happen that Edwards wasn't on guard here?'

'I came in to take a phone message, sir,' Edwards said from behind him.

56

'So he took his chance to slip out and get the car! That's bad, that's very bad. Now they're off and running – we'll put out an alert for them.' He looked at the shotgun. 'At least he dropped this on his way out.'

'He threw it away,' Annie said.

'What?'

'He didn't drop it, he threw it down.'

'Nay ...'

'I can vouch for that,' Sam said. 'I saw him do it.'

Lessiter broke open the gun, expecting to see that it was empty and therefore useless. But there was one cartridge still in the breech. 'We-ell ...' he said. 'I'd best get to the radio. We'll clear out of your parlour, Mrs Sugden. No point now, is there?'

Joe and Matt had come running in the wake of the car's departure. Dolly was hanging on to Matt's arm. They went into the farm kitchen in a clump. 'What happened?' Joe asked. 'We heard a car?'

'They took your mother's car,' Sam explained.

'Oh aye?' Joe said, looking startled. He exchanged a glance with Matt. Matt shrugged. 'Well, Grandad, you all right?'

'I'm fed up of folks asking me if I'm all right,' Sam snorted. 'How can a man be all right at a quarter to six in the morning and no breakfast inside him yet?'

When the policemen had gone, promising to let them have statements to sign later, Sam said: 'Somebody ought to let Mr and Mrs Coulter know their daughter's on the run with Steve Hawker.'

Everyone paused in the business of beginning on the morning meal. Eyes turned to Annie.

She shook her head. 'It would be worst of all, coming from me,' she said. 'The police will tell her.'

'That's hard,' Sam muttered. 'To hear it like that ...'

'I think I ought to ring Mr Hinton, though,' she continued. 'He's really worried about Pip, after the accusations Mrs Coulter was making to him last night.'

'Wait till you've finished your breakfast, lass,' Sam said.

But when she rang him later, the vicar didn't reply.

He was out in Verney's Woods capturing a moth for his collection. He had put up the light trap the previous night, as a distraction to his mind after the unkind interview with the Coulters. He had had little hope of finding anything in it, but there she was: a female herald moth, not particularly rare but nicely shaded, a good example to add to his collection.

He put her in a matchbox and set off for home. In the village street he saw a figure clad in black, a rather sombre, spare man with a mop of soft black hair. Hinton hastened his step to catch up with him.

'Excuse me,' he said.

The man turned.

'I believe you represent an organisation known as the Church of the Word?'

'Do you think of your church as an organisation?' Paul Pangrave countered.

Hinton paused. 'As an organisation for worship – yes.'

'The Church of the Word is a Community,' Pangrave said with simple solemnity, 'not for worship only but for the conversion of the world to the true Word of God.'

'To the exclusion of all other interpretations of that Word?'

'There is only one true Word,' Pangrave replied.

Hinton suppressed a sigh. 'I wanted to speak to you,' he said, 'because –'

'Because you feel I am disturbing your parishioners from their conventional beliefs?'

'Because,' the vicar continued with calm dignity, 'one of your congregation. Mrs Coulter, is in great trouble and needs your help.'

'Ah,' said the preacher. 'Mrs Coulter ...'

'She came to see me last night, not quite herself from worry and grief. Her daughter ... Well, it is best if you hear it from her own lips. I hope you'll be able to bring her some comfort.'

'I shall do my best. But remember the saying: I came not to send peace, but a sword.'

'Ah,' said Mr Hinton, 'that has always proved to be one of the most difficult of Our Lord's sayings for me to understand. However, I trust you won't think of it in connection with Mrs Coulter. She has enough to contend with, without swords.'

Pangrave examined his face, and saw the glint of humour there. He smiled. 'I sometimes find a "sword" more useful in dealing with difficult worshippers than mildness,' he explained.

'Indeed?' Hinton said absently, as if he were listening to something else.

58

'May I be forgiven for saying so, but Mrs Coulter has been a burden to me ever since I arrived in the district –'

'Ssh!' cried Hinton.

'Mr Hinton! I thought you wished to join me in helping –'

'I do, I do, but wait a moment. Don't you hear something?'

'I beg your pardon?'

'Voices?'

Pangrave stared at him dubiously.

'No, truly, Mr Pangrave – I don't imagine I'm Joan of Arc. Can't you hear it? It's not my imagination, surely?'

The preacher came to Hinton's side and cocked his head, listening. They were standing almost on top of the trap door in the pavement outside the Woolpack.

From beneath their feet came a wailing duet: 'He-elp! He-e-elp!'

The story lost nothing in the telling when Amos was able to give his version. And even allowing for a certain amount of dramatic licence, certain facts remained: the owners of the Woolpack Inn had been held up at gunpoint by a young pair, a lad and (according to Henry) a girl, who had used a shotgun to threaten them. Shown the shotgun left by Steve Hawker at Emmerdale, Henry had no hesitation in identifying it.

Sergeant Lessiter found a grim satisfaction in the verification of his suspicions. He said to Annie: 'Well? You were so sure he'd committed no crime.'

Annie bent her head. 'I was wrong,' she said. 'Poor lad. Poor lass.'

To his own surprise, Lessiter was quite upset by her distress. 'Well, any road,' he said, 'you disarmed him.'

'Me?'

'You're not going to tell me he threw down that gun off his own bat.' He glanced at Annie and then away. 'I'm not going any further into it, mind – but a car is a less lethal thing than a shotgun, to my way of thinking.'

Annie made no reply. She couldn't help but feel guilty. She had rescued her father from a perilous situation but what had she done by that act? She had sent a little slip of a girl off into the blue in the company of a lad who had robbed two of her best friends at gun point.

How she would ever face Mrs Coulter if she knew, Annie couldn't imagine.

CHAPTER FIVE

Beckindale could hardly believe so much drama had taken place within its confines, but Amos took care to let them know of it. He did a special piece with pictures for the *Hotten Courier*, which took him back into favour after a slight coolness over a possible libel action. The same story, with variations, was sold to the nationals. Fame had come to Amos at last. It was almost worth being held up at gunpoint.

Emmerdale settled down to normal life quite quickly. Annie's father refused to admit he'd been in any way alarmed by his experience: 'Nay, lass,' he said to her, 'they weren't goin' to harm an old josser like me – what good would it've done them? My main worry was the harm that would be done to *them*.'

'Aye,' she agreed with a sigh. 'And still will be done – and the worst of it is, they're doing it to themselves. How Pip Coulter ever got herself involved in a thing like that, I'll never understand.'

'It's that mother of hers,' Joe insisted. 'She was driven to it.'

'Now, Joe, nobody is ever driven to threatening innocent people with a gun. But I will agree her mother has been no help to her in whatever situation the poor lass was in.'

Annie tried to speak to Mrs Coulter about it, but Pam Coulter had withdrawn beyond a veil of offended silence. She seemed to blame everyone else for having been there to take part as victims in that sequence of events. Sergeant Lessiter murmured to Annie that Mrs Coulter was saying her daughter must have been forced to take part in the robbery – 'But it's not so,' he sighed. 'Amos and Mr Wilks agree that the lass wasn't under duress at any point.'

'No, but she was under the boy's influence,' Annie suggested. 'I mean, she'd never have done it wi'out persuasions from Steve Hawker.'

'Hmm,' Lessiter said. 'That father of his is a bad influence, of course.'

'Never been charged wi' owt like robbery, though?'

'No. Always managed to steer clear of the law.'

'Betty Hawker's never been able to do a thing wi' him,' Annie said. 'I remember t'old vicar – Mr Rosewell – tried to hint to her that Tom Hawker would be a poor match, but she wouldn't listen. She were head over heels in love with him. Seems funny, doesn't it?'

'Aye,' the sergeant agreed. 'Life's full of funny jokes like that, though ...'

Though there was a hunt out for the youngsters, no sign was found. Nor was Annie's car sighted. After the first few days of marvelling and discussing, the subject faded from the conversation.

This was the more so at Emmerdale because personal problems were looming there. Dolly's mother wasn't the easiest person in the world. She might say she approved of Matt, and indeed showed a certain respect, but she intended to have her own way about the wedding.

'I've got a friend in Darlington who's just the person to design your dress, Dolly,' she told her one evening as they sat in Dolly's room at Emmerdale. 'It's got to have a train, of course, so that Lucilla can carry it –'

'Lucilla?' Dolly interrupted. 'Where does she come into it?'

Mrs Acaster eyed her with some sternness. 'She'll be junior bridesmaid,' she said. 'And for your own bridesmaid you'll –'

'Mother, Matt and I are having a quiet wedding. No bridesmaids, no fuss, nothing like that –'

'We won't have any of that nonsense, Dorothy,' replied her mother. 'Your little cousin is looking forward to the chance of being bridesmaid –'

'But I haven't ever seen her but twice or three times in my whole life. And she isn't really my cousin –'

'She's a member of the family –'

'Second cousin twice removed!'

'I've already told her she can carry your train for you –'

'But I'm not having a train –'

'Now, Dorothy, you told me you wanted a proper wedding in a church, which means –'

'It doesn't mean a train! All I want is a white wedding,

61

with a few friends as witnesses –'

'A white wedding?' gasped Mrs Acaster.

'Yes, of course, this is the first time I've ever been wed and I want –'

'Dorothy! You wouldn't go into church a living lie?'

'What?'

'Wearing white? No daughter of mine is going to tell a blatant untruth before the altar –'

'Mother, how can it be untruthful to marry Matt in church? When the bit is read about "let or hindrance" no one's going to speak up. There's nothing to prevent –'

'I'm not speaking about legal untruths, Dorothy. I'm talking about the state signified by a white wedding gown.' Mrs Acaster's sharp, handsome features were tinged with colour. 'You cannot go into the wedding service in a white dress –'

'Mother!'

They faced each other. They had been sitting on the bed, fashion magazines lying between them as they studied styles for the dress. Now both sprang up and there was enmity between them.

Mrs Acaster sought for words. 'Dorothy, you know as well as I do that white is a sign of purity. Can you really tell me your life has been up to standard of a pure white gown?'

'But nobody thinks of it in those terms nowadays –'

'*I* think of it that way! I won't have you walking down the aisle pretending to a character you haven't got –'

'Mother, that's a very cruel thing to say –'

'It's true, and you know it! You ought to realise that if you begin your married life with an acted lie, you're making a very poor beginning.'

'But ... you don't understand – Mrs Sugden is expecting a white wedding –'

'What Mrs Sugden expects is neither here nor there. *I* expect you to live by standards you were brought up to. You made a mistake once – that's in the past now, I admit, but it casts a shadow. You must not come into church in a white dress, Dorothy. If you do, I shall refuse to come to the ceremony.'

'Mother, you can't –'

'I mean it, Dorothy. There are other colours you can wear for a full-scale wedding gown –'

'Other colours? You want me to wear scarlet, happen!'

'Don't let's be absurd, my dear. You always have had a tendency to exaggerate. Once we've settled on a design we can –'

'Mother, I've set my heart on a white wedding –'

There came a tap on the door. Matt put his head round. 'Ma says there's a cup of coffee ready in t'kitchen,' he announced. His rounded, quiet features showed a faint concern; the sound of the quarrel had been audible to him as he came upstairs.

Dolly turned quickly to the door. She was glad of the interruption. Once again she'd been on the verge of a big, useless scene with her mother. Would she never learn that it was pointless to get upset when face to face with her? Mrs Acaster had a will of steel; she would never give in. When she said she wouldn't attend the ceremony if Dolly wore white, she meant it. They might argue till they were hoarse but nothing would change her mind. So it was best to put the matter by for the moment.

Annie could see there had been trouble as they came into the kitchen. She stifled a sigh. Ever since Mrs Acaster appeared on the scene, Dolly seemed to have nothing but trouble.

Annie poured the coffee – good fresh-roasted real coffee, in Mrs Acaster's honour. She offered slices of Ryedale cake. Everyone occupied the moment by sipping and munching.

'Chosen a style yet?' Annie inquired.

'Not yet. It's a big decision,' Mrs Acaster replied. 'I have this friend in Darlington who can design and make the dress –'

'I saw a pattern in a book in Bradford,' Dolly broke in. 'It would be easier to have the dress made from a –'

'I should hope for something a little better than a fifty pence pattern, Dorothy!'

'Fifty pence? Anybody can tell it's a long time since you bought a paper pattern, Mother. More like two pounds, this one was.'

'Even so, anybody could buy it. I should think you'd want something unique.'

'There's really no problem about the dress –'

'Now, my dear, let's be honest about that –'

'I've had quite enough honesty for one day, Mother. I've told you –'

63

'What you haven't told me,' Mrs Acaster cut in, putting down her coffee mug with unnecessary firmness, 'is the actual date of the wedding. That affects the choice of style and material.'

'We're still discussing that. There's a lot to consider –'

'Really? I should have thought you just have to look at the calendar –'

'It's not quite as easy as that, Mrs Acaster,' Annie took it up, seeing Matt look taken aback at the sharpness of the exchange. 'We all want to be in church, you see, but on a farm that isn't simple to arrange.'

Mrs Acaster cast up her eyes, as if to say: 'What else could you expect of farmers?' Aloud she said, 'Well, I take it you have a provisional date in mind. And arrangements are going forward – I mean, the banns are going to be called, and so forth.'

'I'm seeing t'vicar with Dolly in a day or so,' Matt said.

'That's something. What about booking the choir?'

'The choir?'

Everyone except Mrs Acaster looked surprised. Sam, sitting quietly observant in his high-backed chair, gave a little snort of amusement. Matt said: 'Well, we haven't actually ... er...'

'The choir and the organ. You'd best speak to t'vicar about it.'

'Er ... I suppose so ...'

'Mr Hinton will have things like that in mind when he sees them to arrange about the banns,' Annie said. 'I think t'first thing is to get to that stage. You'll need your birth certificate, Dolly – have you got it?'

'Oh yes, I've had to have it because of filling in job applications in the past.'

'And t'name of t'church where you were baptised,' Sam put in. 'Certificate of baptism if you have one, but most folk lose it. T'name and date will do.'

'Oh yes? I hadn't thought of that.'

'Surely that isn't necessary,' Mrs Acaster said in annoyance.

'Wi' Mr Hinton it is,' Sam insisted. 'He's particular, is Mr Hinton.'

'Utter nonsense,' Mrs Acaster muttered.

Taken all in all, it wasn't an agreeable coffee party. Everyone was relieved when Mrs Acaster said goodbye and returned to Beckindale. Dolly and Matt went out for a walk, while Annie cleared up the mugs and plates.

'That woman's a tartar,' Sam remarked.

'She's ... well, she's got an important post in business, Dad. She's used to giving orders.'

'Not to me, she won't.'

'No, but to Dolly ... Did you get the impression Dolly was upset?'

'She's been upset twice a day ever since her mother showed up!'

'Now, Dad, we're going to be connected by marriage. You're just going to have to learn to put up with her.'

'Huh,' Sam grunted.

But, as matters turned out, he didn't have to put up with Mrs Acaster thereafter. When Dolly went to Beckindale that evening to start work at the Woolpack, she found a little note awaiting her there. 'Called back to Darlington urgently. I'll be in touch. Your Affectionate Mother.'

'Bad news?' Amos inquired, hanging around Dolly as she read it.

Dolly gave him a perplexed smile. 'On the whole, no,' she said.

A gentle calm descended on Emmerdale after Mrs Acaster's departure. It was interrupted from time to time as letters arrived for Dolly. Matt got to the stage where he almost dreaded the postman.

'Taffeta!' Dolly cried, looking up from the sheet of notepaper divided between laughter and tears. 'She's suggesting I should have my dress made of yellow taffeta, and encloses a sketch – look!'

Matt looked. What he saw was a drawing of a dress, like every other dress he'd been shown since the wedding was first discussed. It had a long skirt and some twiddly bits around the shoulders.

'Very nice,' he said helplessly.

'Nice? It's hideous! It would look terrible in plain black crepe, but in yellow taffeta it'll look like something on one of those dolls you win at sideshows. And I look terrible in yellow.'

'Nay, love,' Matt began. 'You look good in anything –'

'Oh, it's just like you to say so,' she interrupted. 'But look at me – with my colouring, the last thing I want is to wear yellow!'

He couldn't quite see why. Her fair, thistle-floss hair was almost yellow in its sunny brightness. As far as he was concerned, to match her hair wouldn't be a bad idea. But women knew best about such things.

'You'll look grand,' he insisted. 'But don't have yellow if you don't want to.'

'I won't,' she promised. 'I made up my mind about my dress ages ago.'

'I don't see it matters all that much, Dolly –'

'Not matter?'

'It's just part of t'trimmings, isn't it?'

'Oh, Matt!'

'Have I said summat wrong?'

She put an arm around him and hugged him. 'Yes, but it's summat right too. And what's so nice about it is, you mean it.'

Sam encouraged Dolly to stick out for a wedding gown of her own choice. 'You'll get your way if you just hold fast,' he told her. 'After all, it's your wedding, isn't it?'

'But I want her there, Mr Pearson! She threatens to stay away if I wear white.'

'Nay,' Sam said, shaking his head, 'she's not one to stay away from a big occasion – she'd hate to miss anything!'

But Mrs Acaster didn't reappear in Beckindale. Dolly became perturbed about it. Although she wanted the wedding to go according to her own plan, she wanted her mother to approve. If she insisted on staying away, the chances were that at the last moment she'd descend on her and change everything.

She was at work in the bar one evening when Sam Pearson came in. 'Dolly,' he said, 'somebody just got off the bus and is asking for you.'

Dolly looked past him towards the door. Couldn't be her mother – Mrs Acaster didn't have to ask where to find her.

A little grey-haired lady of about sixty came in. She was clad in an old-fashioned coat with a shoulder cape. Her shoes were low-heeled and of the kind described as sensible. She had a rolled umbrella in one hand and a small suitcase in the other.

'Aunt Jessie!' exclaimed Dolly, hurrying from behind the bar to greet her.

'So this is where you work?' Aunt Jessie said, looking about without much approval.

'What are you doing here?' Dolly went on, taking her suitcase from her and leading her to a table.

The old lady subsided on a chair. 'Answering a call from the family,' she said. 'What a journey ...'

'Mr Brearley, this is my aunt, Miss Renfrew,' Dolly explained to Amos, who was hovering.

'How do?' Amos said. 'What will you take to drink?'

'Nothing, thank you. I don't hold with mixing business with pleasure.'

'Business?' echoed Dolly.

'Yes, indeed, business. I'm to make it my business to see that this wedding goes on in the way that won't be a disgrace to the family –'

'Mother sent you!' Dolly cried.

'Aye, did she!' Aunt Jessie agreed. 'Gasping and spluttering with asthma – you know what a state she gets into when things don't go just as she wants. By her way of it, disaster was about to strike if someone didn't come and take a hand. So here I am, Dolly, and through no wish of my own, for I'm that busy at the boarding house ... But I'm here with full instructions.' She opened a capacious handbag and took out a sheet of paper. 'Your dress, the guest list, measurements of bridesmaids, menu for t'wedding breakfast, and names of flower arrangers –'

'Aunt Jessie!'

'So let's get home and get started. The sooner I speak to Mrs Sugden the better –'

'Speak to her? But she hadn't it in her mind to have anything on that scale, Aunt Jessie –'

'Well, she'll have to lump it, won't she? Your mother is set on it. Take my bag, Dolly.'

'Take it? Where to?'

'To Emmerdale, of course.' Miss Renfrew wheeled on Amos. 'You'll let Dolly have the rest of the day off, of course.'

'Eh?' Amos began, ready to argue. But at a glance from those sharp blue eyes, he was quelled. 'Of course,' he said.

'It'll be more convenient if I stay at Emmerdale,' Miss Renfrew said as she led the way out with Dolly at her heels, 'and so as not to put upon Mrs Sugden too much, I'll share your room, Dolly.'

Henry Wilks had witnessed all this with some amusement. As Amos turned to him in consternation, he grinned. 'You didn't stand on your rights as employer this time, Amos,' he observed.

'Well, I'll go to the bottom of t'barrel ...' groaned Amos. 'Runs in the family, doesn't it?'

'They certainly seem to have some formidable middle-aged females,' Henry agreed. 'Poor Dolly.'

'Poor us,' Amos said. 'We're not going to get any work out of Miss Acaster while all this is going on.'

'Oh, it could be worse,' Henry told him. 'Miss Renfrew might have demanded accommodation here.'

Amos stared at him, aghast. Henry patted him on the shoulder. 'Be thankful for small mercies,' he urged.

'Aye, you're right,' Amos said in a hushed voice.

Other eyes besides Henry's had viewed this episode with some entertainment. Two strangers were settled at a table in a corner of the bar, taking their time over a glass of local ale. A man and a woman – or, in Amos's view, a gentleman and a lady – they had arrived by car half an hour ago. The woman rose now and came to the bar, carrying their glasses for a refill.

'Same again?' Henry asked, stepping forward to fill Dolly's role.

'Yes, please. Very pleasant ale, this.'

'Glad you like it. It's popular with our regulars.'

She looked at the newspapers artlessly folded on the bar top, the newspapers that contained the report by Amos of the robbery at the Woolpack. 'You had some excitement here,' she remarked.

'Too much,' Henry said, watching the ale swirl into the first glass.

'We saw it in the nationals, my husband and I,' she went on. 'Pictures of the pub – with some of your customers, standing outside.'

'Oh aye. They sent a man from London to take those.' Henry picked up the second glass. 'Happen it'll have been worth while just for the advertisement,' he joked, 'if it brings customers from all over t'country.'

'Those men in the photograph,' she said. 'Do they come in often?'

'Eh?' Henry had by now filled the glasses and put them within her reach. He drew one of the newspapers towards him.

'Oh, aye, all of 'em. Almost every day.'

Amos had been longing for a way to break into the conversation. 'I can truly say,' he announced, 'that t'Woolpack has a very faithful clientele. Despite the fact that we'd been the target of an armed robbery last month, our customers never turned their backs on us.'

'Shows how much they value the place,' she remarked. She had somehow spread out the carefully preserved newspaper so that the photograph was on display. 'Local men, are they?'

'Aye.'

She laid her finger under a particular figure in the picture. 'And where does *he* live?' she inquired.

Henry followed the pointing finger. Amos craned his neck.

Then they both frowned and glanced at one another.

For this stranger, this expensively clad woman from who knew where, was pointing to Matt Skilbeck.

CHAPTER SIX

When the phone rang in the kitchen of Emmerdale Farm, Annie was far from imagining that anything unusual was about to happen. 'It's for you, Matt,' she called.

Matt was upstairs changing so as to take Dolly back to the Woolpack. After the surprise of Aunt Jessie's arrival and the discussion that had followed, his one desire was to take a quiet walk with Dolly to work things out. He pushed his feet into his shoes and went somewhat unwillingly downstairs. If it was Peter Hoverden phoning about a Fell Rescue exercise, he'd try to beg off. What he needed was a bit of peace and quiet.

'Hello?' said a light, femine voice on the phone. 'Is that Matt Skilbeck?'

'Yes, speaking. Who's that?'

'Matt! This is Polly!'

'Polly?' Matt repeated. 'Polly who?'

'Polly! Your Polly, Matt! Polly Partridge!'

There was a silence in the farm kitchen that spoke more loudly than words. Dolly, tidying up after the cup of tea served to Aunt Jessie, turned in surprise to look at him. Annie too was watching him. Even Sam, busy with a piece of carving, had stilled his hands.

'*Polly!*' cried Matt.

'How are you, Matt? It's so marvellous to hear from you after all this time! I –'

'Polly! Where are you?'

'I'm at the Woolpack –'

'But – but how d'you happen to be there? I thought you were in Australia –'

'Tasmania, Matt –'

'I thought you were settled there –'

'I was, but now I'm –'

70

'You're at the Woolpack? But that's great. That's just great!'

'When can we meet – ?'

'Wait there!' he exclaimed. 'I'll come and fetch you!'

He slammed back the receiver. His hands were trembling. Annie, astounded, had to admit she had never seen him so overset by anything, excepting only the terrible time when his children were killed. And that was totally different because it had been the extreme of grief. Now, for perhaps the first time ever, she saw Matt in the grip of happy excitement.

'I'm going down to t'Woolpack,' he announced. 'Shan't be a minute –'

'But Matt – I'm coming too –'

'Nay. Bide there. This isn't a night for you to be working at t'Woolpack. Polly's come back!'

'Matt –!'

But he was gone. They heard the Landrover start up. The three in the kitchen stared at one another.

'Who's Polly?' Sam inquired.

He and Dolly looked at Annie, as being the one who knew most about Matt. But Annie had to shake her head. 'I've no idea,' she said.

Matt had never talked about his past much. Naturally, when he asked permission to marry Peggy Sugden, her father Jacob had wanted to know about his family, and at that time Annie had learned that Matt was an orphan, brought up in a children's home from the age of eight after the death of his mother from virus pneumonia. His father had been killed some years earlier in a tractor accident on Hepworth Farm in Ribblesdale. There being no money to finance his education he had gone straight from school into farmwork at fifteen. All his employers had given him good references, his character was of the best according to their letters. He had been farm labourer at Emmerdale for two years before becoming engaged to Peggy and in that time had proved himself a pillar of strength in the face of Jacob's ill temper and lackadaisical outlook.

There had never been the slightest mention of a girl in his life. Annie was at a loss.

The more so as the girl must be important to make Matt so excited.

Sounds overhead told them that Aunt Jessie had finished

unpacking and was coming downstairs. 'My,' Dolly breathed, 'it never rains but it pours, doesn't it?'

'Never mind, lass,' Annie comforted her, 'we'll cope.'

To help do so, and because Matt was obviously about to bring a visitor back with him, Annie went to the larder to take a tray of Maids of Honour from the shelf. Something prompted her to get out the best tea service. Dolly, watching her, looked perplexed. Annie had never got the best tea service out for Dolly! The whole thing was disturbing and odd.

'That looks nice,' Aunt Jessie remarked, as the table was set. 'Expecting company?'

'Seems so.'

Aunt Jessie put away the list of wedding arrangements she'd just got out. 'We'll do this later,' she murmured.

'Aunt Jessie, I don't want to do it at all,' Dolly said. 'I told Mother – all I want is a quiet wedding with a few friends.'

'Now, girl, talk sense. Your mother is never going to go along with that. She'd feel she was letting herself down. If any of us are to get any peace, you'll have to fall in with at least some of her wishes.'

'E-eh,' sighed Dolly. 'I thought weddings were supposed to be happy times?'

Aunt Jessie's reply was lost as the sound of the Landrover was heard. 'That was quick,' Annie remarked.

'He's in a hurry to show her off to us,' Dolly said, with a little shake of her head at her own unkindness.

The door opened and Matt ushered in a young woman about two years his senior. Her clothes, at Dolly's estimation, cast the equivalent of a year's wages. Even her cosmetics were expensive; the faint perfume that hung about her was a guarantee of that.

'This is my cousin Polly Partridge as was,' Matt introduced her. 'Polly Ferris she is now, she tells me. From Tasmania.'

'Your cousin?' Annie cried, coming forward to shake hands warmly. 'I never knew you had any cousins, Matt!'

'It never came up. Polly went away when I were about fourteen – Uncle Ned got a job on an apple farm in Austral – I mean Tasmania ...'

'You can tell by the way he doesn't know the place name that we completely lost touch,' Polly said. 'How do you do,

Mrs Sugden. Matt's been telling me about you on the way here. And this is Dolly, the bride to be.' The newcomer drew Dolly towards her and gave her a little hug. 'I'm thrilled to meet you! Fancy arriving just in time for a wedding!'

The story that emerged as they sat over the tea cups was simple enough. Matt's only relations had been the Partridge family, his mother's brother. Edward Partridge – Uncle Ned – had left Yorkshire fifteen years ago for the sake of his wife's health, and had done well in Tasmania. He was, Matt had just learned, the owner of a thriving apple orchard near Burnie. His daughter Polly had married an English lawyer who had come to visit relations five years ago. Alec had taken a post in Hobart for some years but they were now in England. Pure luck had brought Matt's picture on to the pages of the national newspapers and 'I couldn't mistake him!' Polly cried.

'Same goes for you,' Matt said. 'I knew you the minute I saw you! But why didn't you keep in touch after you left Yorkshire?'

'But I did!' she insisted. 'I wrote, but you never replied.'

Annie sighed. 'I bet the farm didn't bother to send on his letters,' she suggested. 'It's always a problem with men who've had living-in jobs. If you don't re-address letters the minute they come, they get covered up by the other stuff that comes through the post to farmers, and one day you find the letter and you're ashamed to send it on because it's so old ...'

'I suppose that's what happened,' Polly agreed. 'No use crying over spilt milk ...'

'It's marvellous to have you here, any road,' Dolly said.

'Oh, and you wait till I write and tell the others there's a wedding! They'll all be on the next plane.'

'All the others?' Matt replied. 'Who, for instance?'

'Well, Dad, for one. And my stepmother Angie. And Dad's cousin Martin – surely you remember Uncle Martin?'

Matt shook his head.

'All the better then! You'll be amazed at all the uncles and aunts you've got.'

Matt looked happily dazzled. All his life he'd thought of himself as alone in the world, but now all of a sudden he had a family – and a large one at that.

'When are we going to meet your husband?' Annie asked.

73

'I thought he'd have been here by now,' Polly replied. 'I felt we ought not to come together – it was bad enough for Matt having to catch up with me and my news without bringing a husband. But he said he'd follow in about an hour. You don't suppose he's got lost on the way, do you?'

'Not he,' Sam said. 'Henry's looking after him, you said – they've got into talk, I expect.'

That was exactly the case. Henry was trying to find out what Alec Ferris did for a living. There was something about him that was very familiar, but he couldn't quite put his finger on it. For his part, Alec seemed to be purposely obtuse when Henry left openings for him to state his calling. Yet it was clear he was a man of importance. He was wearing a very fine tweed jacket, superbly tailored and with excellent brogue shoes. His speech was cultured and easy yet precise. And this impressive stranger was cousin-by-marriage to Matt Skilbeck.

No use denying it, Henry was impressed. He'd always valued Matt, as a man; but there had always been a feeling of being superior to Matt, not in any unkind way but because Matt made no claims, had no background that called out his status.

Now Henry learned that Matt had relations in Tasmania who seemed to have their share of money. His cousin, Polly Ferris, was a girl of taste and education. Polly's husband counted for something in the world, that was easy to see. All in all it gave Matt additional importance as partner in Emmerdale Farm Limited.

'My wife and I had a look around as we were driving here,' Alec said. 'How much of the land around here is Emmerdale?'

'South of the river, west up the dale to Grey Top, and those ley fields on the east of the main road into the village. Around three hundred acres in all so far, though we plan to buy more as and when.'

'Mostly milk production?'

'And sheep. Matt's the expert on sheep. He's won prizes.'

'Has he, indeed?' To Henry's delight, Alec looked very impressed.

They'd become so interested in their conversation that they hadn't noticed the passing of time. Alec looked up from his sherry to note the time on the Woolpack's clock, and sprang up. 'I've got to get going! I promised to join Polly at Emmerdale.'

'Yes, I bet they're wondering what happened to you,' Henry agreed with some reluctance. He'd been enjoying himself. He didn't really want to part with his new acquaintance. But he couldn't ask to go with him to Emmerdale. Dolly wasn't here, and Amos would blow his top if Henry disappeared too.

The evening was well gone and closing time was approaching when Joe Sugden came in. He'd been to Hotten for a meal with a casual girl-friend, but he didn't look very cheerful.

'Summat up?' Henry asked as he drew his beer for him.

'You could say so.' Joe sipped then put the tankard down and pushed it about a little on the bar top. 'I dropped in at Hotten Police Station before I headed for home,' he said. 'I generally do that if I'm in the town.'

'Aye, we want to get news of your ma's car,' Henry agreed. Then he frowned at Joe. 'There's news?'

Joe nodded. 'They found the car on the outskirts of Liverpool.'

'Liverpool?'

'Liverpool. The sergeant says he thinks it's only a matter of time before they pick up Pip and Steve.'

'How so? Liverpool's a big place.'

'That's just it. They had to pack the car in quite a long way out, so now they're on foot. If you remember, we worked out that they hadn't got all that much cash from the robbery . . .'

'Nay, nobbut eighty pounds or thereabouts.'

'And they've been gone over three weeks. They wouldn't get far with eighty quid, would they? Not now they can't sleep in the car.'

'I see,' Henry said, nodding in comprehension. 'They'll have to get lodgings.'

'So Lessiter thinks they'll nab them soon.'

Henry studied Joe. 'You don't seem very pleased about it.'

'That's the point. I don't know whether I want them to be caught.'

'Now come on, Joe. They held us up with a gun and robbed us!'

'Yeah,' Joe said. 'But you see, I used to give piggy-back

rides to Pip Coulter when she was a little lass at school. I just can't see her ... as a criminal.'

They stood in silence for a time. Then Joe drank up his bitter. 'Well, I'd best drop in at Emmerdale and tell Ma her car's coming back. Promised Lessiter I would.'

'I'd leave it for tonight,' Henry said. 'There's been a lot happening at Emmerdale today!'

The talk in the farm kitchen had turned, with Alec Ferris's arrival, to the pleasant prospect of the wedding. It had been settled that Matt and Dolly would ask the vicar to proclaim the banns for the first time next Sunday, and there was even some discussion about who should give away the bride. Annie took it for granted it would be Henry Wilks.

'You'd best ask him tomorrow,' she remarked to Dolly. 'Unless some member of your own family is coming to take on that role?'

Dolly coloured a little. In the midst of the happy hubbub about Matt's new-found relatives, she was more keenly aware than ever how few of her own would take part in the wedding celebrations. It looked as if her mother had decided to put forth an ultimatum through Aunt Jessie: Unless the arrangements were carried out according to her orders, Mrs Acaster and the other members of Dolly's family would not be attending.

Next day she got back to her normal routine at the Woolpack. But her mind was so full of the interview she and Matt were going to have with the vicar about the date of the ceremony that she forgot to ask Henry if he would give the bride away. When she left the inn after midday closing, Amos turned to Henry.

'Her and Matt are going to see Mr Hinton about the arrangements, are they?'

'That's it, Amos. They're about to make the great leap.'

'I ... er ... I wondered if anything had been said to you about ... er ... the ceremony?'

'Me? Why should anything be said to me? It's their business.'

'No, I mean, Mr Wilks ... about details, like. We all want to play our part in the great event, don't we?'

'Do we? Can't say I'm all that keen, really,' Henry said. He was feeling low today. He felt on the fringe of things at the moment. Matt, young and optimistic, was centre stage for the time being. Henry felt his own day was past; he felt a has-been.

The truth was, he'd drunk too many whiskies with Alec Ferris the previous evening and was suffering from a mild hangover which he knew he ought to cure by a brisk walk in the open air.

'I feel I have a particular interest in Miss Acaster, being her employer,' Amos remarked.

'That's true. I hope you're going to do something handsome by way of a wedding present.'

'Oh, heck!' groaned Amos. 'I've never even thought about that yet!'

'Well, if the banns are to be called next Sunday, we've got three weeks to think about wedding presents.'

'But what should I give Miss Acaster? I mean, I'm closer to her than almost anyone else in Beckindale.'

'You?' Henry exclaimed in astonishment.

Amos looked affronted. 'Why not me?' he demanded. 'I'm her employer. She spends more time in my company than almost anyone else's 'cept Matt Skilbeck. I mean, if we're honest, Mr Wilks, you don't know her as well as I do, even. You're off on your own business such a lot – but I'm practically always here.'

Henry stared at him. He was about to say, 'Rubbish.' But then he paused. In a way, what Amos said was true. In his odd way, Amos took a genuine interest in Dolly. Not to the extent of allowing her to live comfortably under his roof, be it understood – Amos just couldn't be doing with women in his household. But there was no doubt that Dolly had been something special to Amos.

Henry wasn't quite aware how much Amos had done for Dolly. It was thanks to Amos that Matt had been informed of her meeting with Richard at the Feathers Hotel in Connelton, and therefore thanks to Amos that Matt had whisked her away from under Richard's nose.

Amos had offered that information because – to be entirely honest – he didn't want his barmaid to leave Beckindale. But there had been something more. For some strange reason, it had begun to matter to him that Dolly was unhappy, that Matt was unhappy, and that by saying a few words he, Amos Brearley, could make them happy.

He'd had a moment of misgiving when he found Dolly

being kissed by Matt in his own living room the day Matt brought her back. Really, that was quite unseemly! All the same ... They made such a good pair, and they were so alight with happiness and love, and after all Dolly wasn't going to give in her notice and settle down in a little house somewhere with Matt ...

A fondness had grown in him for Dolly and Matt. In a way, they were an ideal pair in his eyes. Matt, quiet and tolerant, would let Dolly go on with her job at the Woolpack. Dolly, quick and bright, would continue to brighten up the bar and cook for Amos and Henry. Amos felt an almost paternal interest in them.

Therefore ... Therefore he felt it would be only right if Dolly asked him to stand at her side and give her away in church.

He would never bring himself to say this aloud to anyone. It was too new, too strange. Fancy him in church, in a new suit, walking down the aisle with Dolly on his arm ... ! But he was getting more used to the idea each time he pictured it, and with the recurring picture came the thought that Dolly might actually ask him. She might, she really might. Why not? He was a respected figure, landlord of the Woolpack Inn, local correspondent for the *Hotten Courier*. Equal to Henry in every way.

Henry wouldn't have agreed that Amos was his equal. We all have a picture of ourselves as being somehow unique, and Henry's uniqueness lay in his estimation of himself as sensible, calm, and discriminating. He was also goodnatured and affectionate, he felt. He was fond of Dolly. It was absurd to say that Amos was closer to her than Henry.

Yet for the first time he looked at Dolly as Amos perhaps saw her. He realised that Dolly was more or less the linchpin of Amos's domestic set-up. Naturally, Amos wanted to give Dolly a good wedding present.

But was there more to it than that? This verbalised claim to be closer to her than Henry ... It was so unlike Amos! Henry became thoughtful. If Amos was actually at the stage where he was thinking of spending money – perhaps a lot of money – on Dolly's wedding present, the whole thing became somehow serious. Henry understood that he must walk with care for a while, until he found out what lay behind Amos's words.

At the vicarage, Mr Hinton was guiding the young couple through the complexities of the marriage arrangements. Matt had been through all this before but had forgotten it. Dolly was new to it and was very nervy. 'It's all right, I assure you,' Hinton told her gently. 'Lots of people go through it and survive.'

Dolly managed a weak smile. 'I know they do. But to have to come into church in front of other folk, and say words at the right time ...'

'All you have to do is respond when I ask you,' he comforted her. 'You're not called upon to make a speech. The big hiatus usually occurs when I ask for the ring and the best man can't remember which pocket he's put it in.'

'I'll put it in Joe's waistcoat pocket myself,' Matt said with a grin. 'That way I'll be able to prompt him if he gets in a muddle.'

Donald Hinton smiled as if in agreement, but in his experience even the calmest of men became jellyfish when they were bridegrooms. 'And who will be giving the bride away, Dolly?' he asked.

'Oh, heck! Beg pardon, vicar,' Dolly added hastily. 'But I quite forgot to do owt about that. Annie reminded me last night I had to see about it.'

'Well, there's plenty of time. I read the banns for the first time next Sunday so you've three weeks. Now let me see. Any other formalities ... ? Oh yes. I hate to be insistent on it, Dolly, but I still haven't had the notification of your baptism.'

'Oh yes. I'm sorry. My mother knew about that when she went back to Darlington and I did expect her to send me the information by now.' Dolly frowned to herself. 'I'll ask Aunt Jessie. Will it be all right if I just bring you the name of the church and the date?'

'Of course. I can then ring the parson now in residence in that parish and verify it.'

'It's important, then?'

Hinton made a little gesture as if pleading for tolerance. 'It's important to me,' he said. 'The marriage ceremony of the Church of England is intended to unite church going members, who have been baptised into the congregation. These days it's thought that anyone can walk into a church and demand to be married, but in fact the priest has the moral obligation to find out that the participants are members

79

of the church. You do understand?'

'Yes, of course, you're quite right,' Dolly agreed. But inwardly she sighed. One more fiddly thing to be attended to. Honestly, she was beginning to wonder if her dream of a white wedding hadn't led her into a lot of trouble. Far simpler just to have a registry ceremony.

But Annie wouldn't like that, she knew. And somehow it seemed the wrong beginning to her new life at Emmerdale.

'Yes, she wanted to be married in the church at Beckindale, with all her friends around her. So she'd have to go along with all the formalities.

That evening, when she returned to the Woolpack for the night's work, she thought Amos was unusually chatty to her. But her mind was elsewhere, busy with thoughts about getting in touch with her mother and making a final decision about the dress.

Her mother was being more than usually difficult. She wasn't at home, or at least if she was, she wasn't answering the telephone. Aunt Jessie wouldn't commit herself on anything without Mrs Acaster's say-so. So now there was a whole list of little problems spread out before Dolly, none of which she could settle because she couldn't get in touch with her mother.

'You'd best write to her, first class post,' Aunt Jessie suggested. 'Put "Urgent" on the envelope. That way she's bound to reply at once.'

'But Aunt Jessie, even if she sits right down, it means two days before we get an answer.'

'That's plenty of time. We can buy the material the day we get her letter. And listen, lass – I'd like the material for the dress to be my wedding present to thee.'

'Oh, Aunt Jessie!' Dolly cried, tears in her eyes at the thought.

'There, there, my lass, don't cry! It's just that I want you to have summat special –'

'And not yellow,' Dolly said, wiping the sparkle from her lashes.

'Nay, but sithee, Dolly. That's a sticking point with your mother. She insists you must not wear white. So I were thinking ... there's lots of shades that aren't white. Besides yellow, I mean.'

'Pardon?' said Dolly.

'I mean, just because your mother doesn't want you in white, that doesn't mean you have to wear yellow.'

'Well, that's true. But I'm not wearing blue either. That's a cold colour.'

'Listen, love, what dosta say to oyster satin?'

'What?' murmured Dolly, suddenly seeing it in her mind's eye.

'With a full skirt. And a nipped-in waist. Bit of a train –'

'No!'

'All right, no train. But lots of width to the skirt –'

'But Auntie Jessie – oyster satin! It'd cost a fortune!'

'That's why I got thee to agree to have the fabric as my wedding present to thee, lass,' Aunt Jessie said with satisfaction.

'Oh, you are a schemer!' Dolly cried. 'But it'd be lovely ... If you think Mother would agree?'

'Listen, my lass, all she's set about is not white. We'll tell her in that letter you're going to write that you've fallen in with her wishes on that point, and urge her to let us know about the other points ... She'll be so eager to give you chapter and verse about what wine to order and so on, she'll let the point about the dress go by. Take my word for it.'

'I said you were a schemer, Auntie Jessie,' Dolly said.

'Well, I've had longer at handling her than you have, lass.'

While Dolly was dealing with her private problems, a greater drama was unfolding. The police arranged for Annie's car to be brought back to Emmerdale through a private garage in Liverpool; it was greeted with pleasure and relief, for the lack of it had made life a little difficult for Annie, with a wedding so near.

The banns were read in church the following Sunday. The Reverend Donald Hinton mounted the pulpit to look out over his congregation with some satisfaction. The church was about half full, a good gathering on a fine sunny morning. The second lesson having been read, he cleared his throat.

'I publish the banns of marriage between Matthew Skilbeck and Dorothy Acaster of this parish. If any of you know cause, or just impediment, why these two persons should not be joined together, ye are to declare it. This is the first time of asking.'

There was a rustle of pleasure among the inhabitants of Beckindale. Heads turned towards Matt and Dolly, who were sitting hand in hand in the Sugdens' pew. Annie, beside them, smiled. Neighbours gave her a returning smile of congratulation.

Joe hadn't turned up for church. This was fairly unusual. He wasn't exactly a pillar of the church but he seldom failed to come to morning service. Annie had told herself he'd probably overslept after a night's jollification in Leeds.

He appeared as they were coming out, to the good wishes of the other members of the congregation. Once again Annie thought he looked rather upset. She left Dolly and Matt and her father with the neighbours, to join Joe as he came up the path.

'Anything wrong, Joe?'

He shrugged. 'Some folk would say not. I dropped in on Sergeant Lessiter last night on my way home. He said Steve Hawker and Pip Coulter were picked up late last night boarding the boat for Ireland.'

'Oh, Joe!'

'They'll be brought to Hotten today, charged tomorrow in Hotten Magistrate's court.'

'Do their parents know?'

'By this time, I expect so.'

He offered his arm and they fell into step to follow the others out of the churchyard. 'Should we be doing anything?' she asked.

'Not as yet. Lessiter said Grandad might be called as a witness when the case goes to trial, but nothing's settled yet – he's hoping they'll plead guilty and save us all a lot of trouble.' He hesitated. 'I'm going to Hotten tomorrow, Ma. I feel I ought to stand by Pip – since I gather her own folks won't.'

'Yes,' Annie said calmly, not voicing her pride at his decision, 'I think that would be a good thing to do.'

The scene in the court next day was very brief. When asked how they intended to plead, both murmured 'Not guilty.' Their legal representatives, appointed by the court since they had none of their own, then asked for bail.

A murmured consultation went on among the magistrates. The chairman of the bench asked the police if they had any objection. Sergeant Lessiter stood up. 'Not to the request on behalf of Philippa Coulter. But as to the youth Stephen Hawker, I would point out that he stole a fire-arm, and

82

discharged it at a police constable, besides using it to effect a robbery and to hold Mr Pearson hostage.'

'Yes, er ... yes, thank you, Sergeant.' Another conference, and then the chairman of magistrates looked down at the two accused. 'We have decided to refuse bail on the request of Stephen Hawker, but are prepared to grant it for Philippa Coulter. However, in regard to the gravity of her case, we set bail in the amount of five hundred pounds.'

There was a gasp of astonishment in the court. Joe saw Pip go pale. Poor kid, she looked thin and hungry and sick. Her usually neat person had a bedraggled air. She'd been living rough for over a month now. Joe couldn't bear the thought of her cooped up yet longer in a police cell.

He got up and hurried to the side of the young lawyer the court had appointed to her.

'Look here, I'll stand bail for Pip Coulter,' he said.

The young man looked round at him. 'Eh?' he said. 'It's a lot of money.'

'But I only have to pay it if Pip skips bail – right? And she won't do that. Will you, Pip?'

She cast him a glance of undying gratitude. 'No, Joe – I won't run away.'

'Very well,' said the lawyer. 'She'll be released to the care of her parents.'

As he drove her home afterwards, Joe wondered if he'd done such a good thing. Her parents hadn't even bothered to turn up in court.

CHAPTER SEVEN

The door of Pip's home opened with great unwillingness to her knock. Mrs Coulter was visible through the crack-like opening. Joe, sitting in his car, watched the exchange that followed. It was clear that Mrs Coulter was telling her daughter she was not welcome. How it might have ended if Joe hadn't been there, he couldn't tell. But looking past her daughter, Pam Coulter glimpsed Joe in the car. Very shame caused her to grab Pip and drag her quickly indoors.

'Huh,' Joe muttered. 'So much for *her* brand of Christianity.'

Annie was eager to hear his news when he got to Emmerdale. He felt obliged to tell her he had stood bail for Pip, but begged her not to mention it to anyone else.

'See,' he said in embarrassment, 'it's a bit funny, i'n't it? She's accused of robbing one of the partners of Emmerdale Farm. It'd look a bit odd to Henry, eh? And if we don't tell Henry, I don't see how we can tell Matt. It'd be like ganging up to keep it from Henry.'

'Aye,' Annie agreed, though with some unwillingness. Through her mind passed that old tag-line of poetry: 'Oh what a tangled web we weave, When first we practise to deceive.' Who had written that? He never said a truer word.

'It'd be all right to tell Grandad,' Joe went on, ''cos I think he's got a soft spot for Pip. But same thing applies to him as Matt – if he should ever let it out to Henry, it'd cause a fuss.'

'But it'll become known, surely. Won't it be in t'paper?'

'Dunno,' Joe confessed. He searched his mind for recollection of court reporting. 'I think they generally just say, "Bail was granted." I don't think they say who stood guarantee.'

'But there were people in court?'

'Oh aye. Quite a turn-out,' he said in a bitter tone. 'Folks like other folks' troubles, I reckon.'

Annie sighed. 'That's human nature. But what I mean is, somebody's sure to mention to someone else that it was you who stood bail.' She hesitated. 'I suppose it's all right? Five hundred pounds is an awful lot of money, Joe.'

'Too true. But Pip isn't going to jump bail. She has to report to t'police every day – at police cottage. She'll do it, never fear.'

'Poor little lass,' Annie said. She was thinking of Pam Coulter's frozen expression whenever she came across her in the village street. Pam Coulter was determined to show by her attitude that she disapproved of her daughter much more strongly than anyone else in Beckindale.

Compared with this domestic tragedy, Dolly's anxiety about her mother's actions seemed almost trivial. She had written to her in Darlington, and received the strangest reply, which she read out to Annie. 'I haven't time for all that now,' she read. 'You'll have to deal with it yourself.'

'Well,' said Annie, 'that's what you wanted, isn't it?'

'Yes ... No ...' murmured Dolly. 'It's so unlike her! Last time we saw her, she was all for managing every aspect of my wedding. Now all of a sudden she's not bothering – she doesn't answer any of the questions I asked, she just don't seem to care.'

'She's always been ...' Aunt Jessie sought for a word. She was going to say 'erratic'. She changed it for 'emotional'.

'Well, I just can't understand it,' Dolly said in a miserable voice.

'If you're worried, happen the best thing is for me to go back to Darlington and see what's what.'

'Oh, would you, Aunt Jessie?' Dolly cried. 'It would set my mind at rest!'

'Think you can manage wi'out me?' Miss Renfrew inquired with a twinkle.

Dolly blushed. 'Oh ... I didn't mean ... But we settled about t'dress ...'

'And, listen, about t'reception,' her aunt said. 'How would it be to have t'wedding in the afternoon, and have an evening reception and dance in t'village hall?'

Dolly gasped. Annie sat back in her chair. A silence followed.

'No?' said Miss Renfrew. 'I thought it were a good idea, myself.'

Dolly looked at Annie. One of her anxieties about the wedding had been that Annie seemed to be shouldering all the tasks usually taken on by the family of the bride. Dolly's mother had at first shown a keen managerial interest but now all of a sudden it seemed she couldn't care less. Annie had stepped in, without fuss. There was a lot still to be done – invitations to get printed, flowers to arrange, catering to book, guest lists to be finalised ... If at least some of the work could be put off on a professional catering firm who would set up the reception at the village hall, matters would be simplified.

'I think it's a grand notion,' Annie said.

Dolly smiled in relief. 'All right then, Aunt Jessie, you go back to Darlington and tell Mother all that. Oh, and by the way, don't forget to sort out that business about the baptism.'

'Oh aye,' Aunt Jessie said.

After breakfast Dolly went up to her room with her aunt to help her pack. At first she had a lot to say, reminding her of this and that to pass on to her mother. But by and by a silence seemed to grow between them.

'What's up, Aunt Jessie?' Dolly asked at last.

'What makes you think something's up?'

'You've gone all quiet.'

'Aye ... well ... old family history makes you turn your thoughts inward.'

'Inward to what?'

'I wonder if you remember ... You were nobbut a little thing ... D'you remember the night your father threw the family Bible on t'fire?'

Dolly's eyes widened. After a moment of surprise she said: 'I'm not likely to forget it! It was the only time I ever saw Mother cry.'

'Good reason, too! That Bible had been in our family over a hundred years – given to our mother by her grandmother – that's great-Grandmother Bertha, you remember?'

'Aye. What about it, Aunt Jessie?'

'I can see it like yesterday,' Miss Renfrew said, turning over in her hands the nightdress she was supposed to be packing. 'The pages rolling up as if they'd been in curling tongs, and going brown and crisp wi' t'heat, till there was nothing left except clinker and t'brass clasp as black as your hat.'

86

'Mother still has that clasp,' Dolly said. 'In her button box.'

'Has she now?' the old lady said with fond regret. 'Ah, your mother had to give in over many a thing wi' your father, Dolly.'

'Oh, Aunt Jessie! She were always getting on at him!'

Her aunt looked startled. 'You remember more about the situation than I'd thought! Aye, they were a pair, I reckon. Your father were that strongly "chapel" that his principles over-ruled almost everything else.'

'Like that Mrs Coulter,' murmured Dolly.

'Who?'

'Never mind. Go on.'

'As long as he lived, your father always insisted on chapel every Sunday. After he passed on, your mother felt free to take you to church. That would be when you were about ... what ... six? Seven?'

Dolly sighed. 'Aunt Jessie, if you're trying to tell me I were never christened into Church of England, I've guessed.'

Her aunt gasped, sprang up, threw the nightdress into her suitcase, and said angrily, 'Then why didn't you say so, instead of letting me rattle on like a fool?'

'I didn't know how to say it. It seems so ... sort of funny. But I don't see what all the fuss is about. I'll just get married and christened in "one fell swoop".'

Her aunt was horrified. 'What, and have strangers pointing the finger? You'll do no such thing! Your mother would die of shame! She's had trouble enough in her life, goodness knows, wi'out having a thing like that to mar the pleasure of the ceremony. I'll tell you this, Dolly,' she said, thumping the bed with her fist, 'your mother will never set foot in t'church if I tell her you're getting christened and wed at the one time!'

Dolly gave up the argument. She and her aunt would have to consult Annie. Annie would know what to do.

In fact, Annie had the solution at the ready. They would speak to the vicar and arrange for a quiet ceremony on a weekday when the church was deserted. Better yet; when they spoke to Mr Hinton, he sympathetically suggested that the ceremony should be conducted in Robblesfield parish so that no one in Beckindale need ever hear of it.

'Well, that's settled,' Annie said as they turned away from seeing Aunt Jessie on to the bus for Hotten and the train to

Darlington. 'Now all you have to do is arrange for Henry to give you away. You haven't asked him yet, have you?'

'I keep forgetting! There's so much to think about, Annie!'

'That's true enough. Well, look, I'm going into t'Woolpack now to give Henry some papers he asked for about the tax situation. I'll ask, shall I?'

'Would you? 'Cos I've got to go up to Grey Top to meet Matt – he promised to show me the ewes he's chosen to show this year.'

Annie nodded. She understood how much Dolly wanted to learn about farming so as to be able to discuss Matt's work with him. For a girl with a town background, there was a lot to learn.

They parted in the square. Annie went into the inn. Henry was upstairs and from various thumps and bumps, Amos was in the cellar. At Annie's call, Henry came down. 'Hello,' he said, and then seeing the folder, 'oh, the tax estimates!' He groaned. 'I suppose I've got to look at them. I promised Joe I would.' He took the folder, opened it, flicked over the first two or three forms, and closed it. 'Bye ... One of the things I *don't* like about life in Beckindale is the multiplicity of forms connected with farming!'

'I'm sorry, I'd do away with 'em if I could.'

'Trouble is, if you accidentally on purpose throw 'em in the fire, they just send you another set.'

She nodded. Henry drew out a chair for her. 'Coffee? I was just about to make some for me and Amos.'

'That would be nice. Henry, I'm here on an errand for Dolly.'

'Oh aye?'

'She wants you to give her away.'

Instead of the instant acceptance she'd expected, Henry hesitated.

'Nowt wrong, is there?' she asked quickly.

'It's a bit awkward ...' He busied himself with the kettle at the sink. Over the rush of the water he said, 'Thing is, Amos has been hinting for a while now, about how he has this closeness to Dolly –'

'Closeness?'

'There's summat to it, Annie.' He put the kettle on the stove. 'He does seem to have a feeling for her.'

Annie nodded. She recalled the time when Amos had come

in great secrecy to Emmerdale, to ask her advice: he knew where Dolly was to be found although she had vanished from Beckindale – should he pass on the information to Matt? It was thanks to Amos that Matt had in the end proposed to Dolly.

'He keeps dropping hints,' Henry said, unscrewing the jar of instant coffee. 'Saying how it's always me that gets the important jobs, and how he has a claim as Dolly's employer – but what he means is he feels he's more fond of her than I am.'

'You mean *he* wants to give Dolly away?' Annie said, truly taken aback.

'Just that.'

'But ... Amos? He'd have to ... I mean, Henry, he'd have to get dressed up for church!'

'Oh aye. He's even ordered a suit.'

'He never has!'

'He has.'

'Oh.'

'Is there owt we can do about it?'

Annie thought about it. 'It's up to Dolly. In the absence of a father, Dolly can choose whoever she likes.'

'But Amos is so forlorn about the whole thing, Annie.' The kettle boiled and Henry poured water on to the coffee in the cups. 'I don't think I could face him if I had to tell him I was Dolly's choice.'

'You're asking me to interfere, aren't you?'

'Not exactly interfere ...'

'It's up to you, really. You can make Dolly miserable by refusing or Amos miserable by accepting.'

'Eh, Annie! You can be blunt sometimes!'

Annie smiled at his concerned expression, at the way he was tugging his bristly moustache in distress. 'I'll see what I can do,' she conceded. 'Now call t'lad up out of the depths for his coffee.'

Annie had let Matt's new-found relations know that they would be welcome to stay at Emmerdale. Now that Aunt Jessie had packed up and gone, it gave her a chance to turn things round a little in preparation for her new guests. She hurried home after her coffee to begin on the cleaning.

Dolly came in from her walk up to Grey Top, looking more settled in her mind than for some days. 'It makes you

89

realise,' she said, 'when you see the moors and the hills, what a lot of turmoil we get into over nowt!'

'"I will lift up mine eyes unto the hills",' Annie quoted. She smiled. 'All the same, weddings are mentioned in t'Bible too.'

'Oh, that's true. Did you ask Henry about giving me away?'

'We-ell, I began to get to the point,' Annie said. 'I didn't actually settle it. What would you do if Henry said no, Dolly?'

Dolly stared, pausing in the act of getting out the paring knife to do the dinner vegetables. 'D'you think he might?'

'Who would you ask if he'd rather not?'

'But Henry wouldn't feel like that, would he?' Dolly cried, much hurt. 'I thought he liked me?'

'Of course he likes you, love. But the thing is ... You see, he gave the bride away at Joe's marriage. And look how badly that ended. Henry sort of feels ... he's not a bringer of good luck.'

'You mean he might refuse because he wants me to have a good start?'

'Something like that.'

'It'd be right embarrassing if I asked him and he wanted to say no.'

'I suppose it would.'

'But he'd say yes, even if he felt like that, wouldn't he?'

'Oh, I think he would. But he'd be a bit bothered, happen.'

'Because he feels he'd be unlucky for me?'

'Could be.' Annie looked thoughtful. 'But there's nobbut Henry you could ask, really. It's got to be someone about that age, hasn't it? And there's no one else you know that well.'

'No.o ...' Dolly agreed. 'He and Amos are the only two, really.' She brightened. 'What if I asked Amos?'

Annie raised her eyebrows as if the idea surprised her, but smiled. 'He'd be absolutely delighted. It's the kind of thing he'd love doing.'

'But what would Henry think?'

'Well, I think ... I s'pose Henry would approve too. He's fond of Amos. It'd please him to see Amos given a chance to shine. But mind –' Annie disappeared into the larder and spoke as a distant voice – 'it's entirely up to you.'

Dolly let the notion simmer for the rest of that day. As

far as she could see, everything to do with the arrangement of the wedding was going wrong. Her mother seemed to have lost interest. Aunt Jessie had rushed away to see what was bothering her, thus leaving Annie with all the work. Henry didn't seem to want to act as father-of-the-bride. Even Mr Hinton seemed to be perturbed about something other than the wedding. He was kind when he spoke to her, but was abstracted, as if his thoughts were really elsewhere.

She sat down with Matt in the Woolpack that evening and some of her worries spilled out. 'Nay,' he said, taking her hand, 'far as I can see, we're doing all right. Ma says she's got it going smooth. There is one thing, though – t'matter of cost –'

'I know,' Dolly said at once, embarrassed. 'My mother should pay –'

'Now don't get bothered! It's all right, I'll see Annie doesn't get out of pocket –'

'Fact is, love, I've decided to forget about my mother. Aunt Jessie got back to Darlington this afternoon and rang me to say Mother's gone – packed a bag and *gone*! Goodness knows where she is.'

'I don't see what you mean, gone?'

'Just gone. She'd watered her plants and given the cat to a neighbour to look after for a week or so.'

'You mean she's gone on holiday?' Matt exclaimed, staggered.

'Looks like it.' Dolly's creamy skin was tinged with colour. But her mouth was rather grim. 'We'll pay Annie back for all she's spending. And Aunt Jessie said she'd help.'

'I don't know as we ought to take anything from Aunt –'

'I feel the same, Matt, and I'll pay her back somehow. But t'fact is, my mother's just vanished into t'blue and I'll have to manage best I can without her.'

'Aye,' Matt said on a note of doubt. 'Well, don't say owt to Ma about money until I've had a think.' He surveyed what else needed to be done. On a more cheerful tack he said, 'Asked Henry to give you away?'

'No,' said Dolly, 'and I don't even know that I'm going to.'

'But I thought it was agreed – ?'

'We did sort of feel ... took it for granted, happen ... but for various reasons I've decided to ask Amos.'

Matt really gaped at her. 'Amos?' he echoed.

'Well, he's been nice to me in his way,' Dolly said, rather too quickly. 'And I'm quite fond of him ...'

'Aye?' Matt said, doubtful.

'And I think he'd like to do it.'

'Aye,' Matt said, imagining the chaos that might ensue if Amos got loose on the wedding ceremony.

'Don't you want him to?'

'Nay, lass ... That's your choice. Not for me to interfere.'

'But I want you to approve,' Dolly said with some intensity. 'I'd not like someone up there at the altar with us, that you didn't like.'

'I like Amos,' Matt said, thinking back to the night when so unexpectedly Amos had changed a cheque for him, against all tradition. Without that money, Matt would have felt a bit at a loss when he walked into the hotel at Connelton to face Dolly and Richard. 'Aye, he's all right. And come to think on it, it'll do Henry no harm to take second place for once!'

Henry would have been amused if he'd heard that, considering it was his own idea to put Amos into the centre of the stage as father-of-the-bride. But Henry was busy in the bar, whereas this conversation was taking place in the back room of the Woolpack.

Amos came in at that moment, to fetch clean drying cloths. He drew back embarrassed at finding Dolly and Matt holding hands. 'Oh, beg pardon,' he exclaimed, backing away.

'Nay, Amos – Mr Brearley!' Dolly cried, raising her voice as he was about to disappear back into the bar. 'Can I speak to you a minute?'

Somewhat apprehensive, Amos returned.

'Can I ask you a favour?' Dolly went on.

He was immediately cautious. 'Ah ... a favour ...' he said. 'What sort of favour? Can't say till I know, can I?'

'I wondered ... I'd like very much ...' Dolly faltered and took a firmer grip on Matt's hand. 'Since I haven't a male relative anywhere near, I wondered ...' She swallowed, suddenly afraid that he too would be unwilling – and what would she do then? 'Would you give me away when Matt and me get married?'

Amos stared at her. He went pink. He raised his eyes for a moment as if he saw rainbow visions overhead. Then he said in a stifled voice: 'At the wedding? Give you away?'

Oh dear, thought Dolly, he doesn't want to. 'It would be a big favour,' she said pleadingly.

'Oh,' gasped Amos. 'Oh heck ...' His face broke into a huge smile. He put his hand on top of his balding pate as if he felt a crown growing there. 'Oh, good gracious, oh heck!' He turned and bolted back to the bar to exult over Henry Wilks.

Dolly sat transfixed. She'd no idea it would mean so much to him.

'Well,' Matt said with dry good humour, 'I suppose that meant he agreed!'

CHAPTER EIGHT

Joe Sugden was getting somewhat unwillingly into his clothes next morning when he looked out of the window at Demdyke. To his astonishment he saw a slight figure in a thin mackintosh trudging along the pavement beyond the patch of grass in front of the cottages.

What the devil was she doing out at this time of the morning?

He thrust the tails of his shirt into his trousers and ran out. She was a little further along the road, walking slowly as if she had no energy.

'Pip!' he called. 'Pip!'

She stopped, turned – but didn't come back towards him.

'Pip!' He ran to join her, but she turned away. He caught her by the shoulder. 'Pip, what on earth are you doing out so early –'

She shrugged off his hand as if to get away.

'Hang on,' he said, worried about her. She was extraordinarily pale. 'I've just got a cup of tea made – come on in and have one.'

'Nay ...'

'Come on,' he said, taking her by the arm. 'I won't bite you.'

'Shouldn't think you'd want to see more of me than you could help,' she mumbled.

'Aw, heck, we all make mistakes ...' He was turning her towards his house. 'Come on up for a cup?' And as she made as if to shake her head he added, 'You can make me a slice of toast while I shave. I'm a bit behind this morning. Woke up late.'

'Missed milking, have you?' she inquired with a faint humour.

'Nay, I knew I were going to have a late night. I made

94

arrangements wi' Matt.' As he spoke he was guiding her up his front path and into the house. She was very cold, her little thin hand was like ice in his.

He got her coat off. It had no warmth in it, would hardly keep out a straw stem if you pushed hard. He shaved with his battery shaver while she fussed about finding bread and butter but when it came to the point, she ate more toast than he did. Eyeing her while she gobbled it down, he understood she was famished. 'I think I fancy a bit o' bacon,' he remarked. 'A slice of toast isn't enough, a sharp morning like this.' He showed her where to find it, and the eggs, and took it for granted she would cook enough for herself so that, in fact, she made a good breakfast.

Somehow he got the impression this was the first meal she'd had in twenty-four hours. It worried him.

Quite easily they began to talk about the predicament she found herself in. She shook her head so that her soft long hair caught on her dress collar. 'It's hard to believe,' she muttered. 'Me! Charged with armed robbery! It don't make sense ...' Then, quickly, as he was about to say something comforting, 'I'm not saying it's not true. It happened. I did it. I did it just as much as Steve. But I can't believe it really happened.' She sighed. 'I can't honestly. It's like a dream.'

'I don't reckon you're a crook,' Joe remarked.

'Nor is Steve!'

'I'd have said not,' he agreed. He hesitated. 'Why did he do it? I mean, Pip ... there must be a reason for a lad to go off t'rails like that.'

She offered no comment so to fill the gap he asked if she'd like more to eat. 'Nay, I've had a good feed,' she said. 'Didn't know I was so hungry. I'd like another cup of tea, though.'

He poured it then began to collect the dirty plates and put them in the sink, talking the while. He thought it best to ease his way into what he really wanted to say, so he told her about Matt and Dolly getting wed, and the appearance of Matt's new-found relations. When at last he got round to asking the question he had in mind, he found she had fallen asleep in the armchair. The fresh cup of tea was on the table nearby, untouched.

So it was no use asking her why she and Steve felt they had to head for Ireland without telling her parents.

He looked at her with compassion. In sleep she looked even younger, and very vulnerable. There were dark shadows under her eyes, her cheekbones were prominent as if she had been under-nourished for some time.

But Joe had to get to Emmerdale. Should he wake her? It seemed downright cruel to do that. After a moment's thought he found an old envelope and printed on it: 'Gone to Farm, see you later. Food in larder, help yourself. Back by noon. Joe.'

He thought it best not to mention his visitor to his mother and grandfather. He wanted to learn more about her plans before he did that; there was something funny about finding her wandering around at seven in the morning outside Demdyke.

He found in any case that no one expected him to talk. All the conversation at Emmerdale was about how Amos had taken to his role of father-of-the-bride. 'He's like a dog wi' two tails,' old Sam reported. 'Henry told me he stayed up till all hours last night reading a book on wedding etiquette.'

'I hope you know what you're doing!' Joe teased Matt. 'He'll likely want to sign the register for you!'

'Nay,' Sam said, 'he's got it all off to a T! He's read the book!'

He surprised Annie by saying he wouldn't stop at the farm for midday dinner. 'Got something I want to see to back at Demdyke,' he said.

'Don't forget to get something to eat, then.'

'No, I won't.' He drove back to Beckindale thinking that he'd get Pip to heat up a tin of stew for the two of them. But when he went into the cottage in Demdyke Row, she'd gone.

She'd washed up all his dirty dishes and left them to drain on the draining board, and put away the marmalade and butter and so forth. The note he'd left propped against the marmalade jar was lying flat on the table. He snatched it up – but she'd added no remarks to it. She'd just walked out.

Well, she had a perfect right to. There was no law said she had to do what Joe Sugden told her to. Yet he was worried. There was something so ... so lost about her. And surely most folk who were in a settled frame of mind would leave a note in reply to his – 'Thanks for the meal but I've gone home' or summat like that.

He went out and hurried round to the lane where the

Coulters lived. He knocked on the door. No reply. But the lace curtain at the window twitched so he knocked again.

'Come on, Mrs Coulter, I know you're there,' he called through the letter box. 'I want to talk to Pip.'

'She's not here,' a voice replied.

'Where is she, then?'

'Mind your own business, Joe Sugden!'

He knocked again and called, but got no further response. Mrs Coulter was too ashamed at what had happened to want to face anyone.

By now thoroughly anxious, Joe went for a walk round Beckindale to see if he could spot Pip. He had a feeling that she was walking around at random. His steps eventually took him past the vicarage, where the vicar was digging his garden.

'Ah, Joe,' he said, straightening with relief as he approached. 'Wouldn't like to volunteer to take this on, would you?'

'Nay,' said Joe, 'I see enough of t'land in my own job.' He glanced about. 'Pip Coulter isn't here, by any chance?'

'Here?' Mr Hinton sighed and shook his head. 'I think this is probably the last place she'd come, Joe. She came here before ... Before that terrible business with the gun at the Woolpack.'

'Did she? I never knew that!'

'Ah, well, a priest isn't supposed to talk about conversations with parishioners ... She was in great distress, asked me to help her. And I let her down, Joe.'

'Well, difficult to help her when her mother and father are against your church ...'

'I should have done more. I should have tried ...' Hinton looked distressed, then collected himself. 'Why do you want her?'

'Fact is, I found her wandering about this morning in my road and gave her a cup of tea. When I left home she was asleep in a chair. Now she's vanished.'

'Gone home?'

'I ... somehow don't think so,' Joe said. 'I went there, and Mrs Coulter wouldn't answer the door. She said Pip wasn't there and I believe her.' Joe gave the vicar a straight glance, 'I thought happen you could go and ask where she's gone.'

Hinton drew back. 'You know I shouldn't be well-received there!'

'But ... vicar ... she looked real bad. Strained, ill ...'

'Anxiety about her fate when the case is heard ...'

'But that oughtn't to make her so tired she's asleep as soon as she's got some grub inside her and sitting in a decent chair!'

'No,' the vicar agreed. 'But if she is ill, Joe – it's up to her parents to care for her. I *want* to help, but I have no authority – especially with a family that are not members of my church.'

'But you'll try?'

Mr Hinton gave a half smile. 'I'll try, Joe.'

The moment Joe had walked away another figure detached itself from the shadows of the trees further up Vicarage Lane. Tom Hawker came into the vicarage garden, gaunt and angry.

'Hey, vicar! I want a word wi' you!'

Hinton had just picked up his spade again. He dug it into the soil as a parking place to turn towards the speaker. His heart sank as he recognised Steve Hawker's no-good father. 'Mr Hawker, isn't it?' he said politely.

'Aye, and well you know it. My missus came to see you yestiday, didn't she?'

The vicar put his hands on the spade as if to resume work.

'Deaf, are you?' Hawker exclaimed. 'I asked you a question!'

'I heard you.'

'Then what's the answer?'

'I have nothing to say to you about whether people have come to speak to me.'

'Oh, that's the attitude, is it?' growled Hawker. 'Then I'll tell you summat, shall I? I want no interfering by you in my family affairs. I can handle them.'

'Can you?' Hinton returned in an unexpected tone of coolness. 'Can you handle Steven's?'

'Aye,' Hawker said, his lantern-jawed face creased with intensity. 'Lookee, vicar! I'm not a man for goody-goody. What's coming to Steve serves him right for taking up wi' a little slut like that Coulter lass. He'll have to take his medicine. But thee keep out of it, understand?'

The vicar studied him with dismay, his brown eyes full of perplexity. 'I almost think you want your son to go to jail,' he murmured.

'It'll teach him, won't it? Allus telling me I wasn't up to much –'

'I'm sure Steven never said –'

'Oh, he let me know it! But I was never in jail, was I? Because I'd more sense than get mixed up wi' the likes o' Pip Coulter. And that brings me back to what I was telling thee at t'outset – my missus came here and don't you deny it. And I've told her, as I tell thee – I don't want no interference in settling what's to be done over Steve.'

'But it's not up to you to settle –'

'We'll see about that, vicar,' grunted Tom Hawker, and lurched away with his shoulders hunched.

Joe had finished his search of the village and then realised that it was almost time to get back to work, but he still hadn't eaten. He stopped at the Woolpack for a half and a pie, hardly hearing Amos as he rehearsed the list of duties that now fell to him in the marriage ceremony.

There was an afternoon's work ahead of Joe. He gave it his attention but part of his mind was always wondering what on earth had happened to Pip Coulter. The vicar rang Emmerdale to leave a message for him; he'd tried to speak to Mrs Coulter, without success. It was a puzzle. Was Pip all right, or not?

As he drove away from the farm after tea with the family, he saw a tiny figure trudging up a slope on Emmerdale land, heading towards an old shed in which Joe kept fodder for sheep in case of hard weather. It was a place to which neither he nor Matt went except to take out supplies to livestock in snowy weather or to renew the stocks about twice a year.

He got out of the Landrover to call. 'Pip! Pip!'

She was too far off to hear, or else the breeze carried his voice away. By the time he set off after her, she'd already gone into the shed.

He found her sitting on a bale of straw, looking exhausted. 'Pip!' he exclaimed. 'What are you doing here?'

She looked at him, too weary to show any other reaction.

'I've been looking for you,' he went on. 'Didn't you see the note I left? Why didn't you wait?'

She hung her head. 'I have to go to the police to report every day. 'Cos of being on bail.'

'Oh aye – that's right. But you could have come back.' He glanced about. There were little packets of this and that on

99

the bales of fodder – biscuits, cheese, a carton of milk. A terrible understanding came to Joe. He said: 'I tried to talk to your Ma. She kept the door shut.'

'The door's shut on me too,' Pip said with bitterness.

'You mean ... she won't let you in?'

Pip nodded.

'You ... living here, then?' He nodded at the food.

'Aye.'

'Had you been out all night when I saw you this morning?'

'I slept here a bit.'

'And what were you planning to do tonight?' When she avoided his eyes he said: 'Were you going to sleep here again?'

'Nothing else I can do, is there?' she said in a quavering voice.

'Aye!' he said. 'You can come wi' me.'

'But I –'

'No buts. Come on.' As she tried to pull away from him he said fiercely, 'Heck, Pip, we're old friends. I've known you since you were in kindergarten. You don't think I'm going to leave you to kip down here wi' only those odds and bobs to eat? There's bags of room at Demdyke.'

'Oh, Joe,' groaned Pip as he helped her up. 'And it was your gun Steve stole!'

'Aw, forget about that,' he replied, putting his arm about her to help her out of the shed. 'Come on.'

'But ... but ...'

'Either you come home wi' me or I stay here the night wi' you,' he told her, half-laughing and half-serious. In response she tried to smile, but then her eyes seemed to glaze over for a moment. She didn't faint, but it was as if her senses swam when she got up.

With Joe's arm about her she went out of the barn. Neither she nor Joe saw the figure lurking in the lee of the stone wall at the foot of the pasture. Tom Hawker had made it his business to find Pip Coulter and keep an eye on her.

Joe took her in the Landrover to his cottage at Demdyke and settled her in with a fire going in the grate. She seemed to be chilled through, too exhausted to keep herself warm without help. When she had a hot drink and a bite to eat, he hurried off to tell Mr Hinton the news.

'I thank God you've found her,' the vicar said, meaning

it literally. 'Steve's father was here earlier today, making what sounded like threats against her.'

'Threats? How d'you mean?'

'He holds her entirely to blame for what happened. He was muttering that he'd "settle" accounts. I don't like it ...'

'Oh, you don't want to pay any heed to him. He's allus been a pain in the neck, Tom Hawker. Never keeps a job for more than four days together because he gets across with anybody he works with. Allus going to make a fortune wi' some horse he's picked, but it never comes off. He's a dead loss.'

'Mmm,' said the vicar, not inclined to write him off so easily. 'All the same, Joe – I'd tread carefully about this thing.'

'How d'you mean?'

'Well, in the first place, you're giving shelter to a girl against whom you may have to give evidence in court –'

'Not against, vicar. I'm not against Pip –'

'The evidence cannot be in her favour, now can it, Joe? You saw her help to take your grandfather hostage –'

'Hostage!' Joe cried. 'He were only in that shed half an hour and were having the time of his life, being the centre of interest.'

'Now, now! The fact that he came to no harm is not the point. Pip and Steven took him as hostage. And you will have to say so. Now here you are, giving a home to the criminal –'

'Pip's no criminal.'

'I agree with you, but think how odd it might look to the authorities. Then there's the point that she is an unmarried girl –'

'Aw, come on, vicar! I've known Pip all her life. She's like a kid sister to me.'

'Yes but ... There's something you don't know.'

'What?'

'I don't know whether I ought to tell you.' The vicar pulled at his long upper lip. 'But since you've involved yourself so thoroughly, I think you have to know. This is in confidence, Joe.'

'Go on.'

'Steve Hawker's mother came to see me yesterday, to ask my advice. She'd had a letter from Steve, from prison. Pip is expecting his child.'

Joe stood staring at the vicar. After a moment he drew in a slow breath. 'So that's why she looks so ill ...'

'Does she? You must remember, I've scarcely seen her.'

'Oh, she looks right poorly. And nearly passed out when I found her in t'barn. Oh, aye, I should have guessed!'

'I hardly think it's a thing you'd guess –'

'And that's why she and Steve were running away!' Joe broke in. 'Of *course*! That's why they needed money! They knew they'd never get permission to get wed from her folks – good heavens, when you think of t'way they carry on about little things ...'

'I think you're right,' the vicar acknowledged. 'I ought not to make judgements, but I can't help feeling that if Mrs Coulter had been less hard on her daughter, Pip wouldn't have thrown herself into a love affair with Steve and found herself pregnant. I do feel –'

'And that's why she's been turned out!' Joe hastened on. 'She's broke the news to Mrs Coulter and Mrs Coulter's shown her the door. So much for her religion!'

'Joe, I don't think we ought to –'

'I tell you, it makes me see red!' Joe snorted. 'That poor little lass –'

'But you do see, don't you, that you must watch out what you're doing. I don't think, for instance, that you ought to sleep at Demdyke tonight – not with Pip in the same house.'

'Uh-huh,' said Joe. 'I see it's a bit awkward. I suppose I could go up to the farm – though it'll be a bit of a squash now Ma's giving hospitality to this cousin of Matt's and her husband.'

The vicar looked as if he felt he ought to offer Joe a room at the vicarage, and seeing the thought forming in his mind Joe hastily amended his views. 'It'll be okay,' he said. 'Dolly's moved in wi' Ma for the time being so's Matt's cousin can have her room, so I daresay I can move in wi' Matt or Grandad just for the one night.'

There had been so much pressure on bedroom accommodation that Dolly asked Amos if she might stay a couple of nights at the Woolpack. Normally Amos would have refused, but he now felt *in loco parentis* to Dolly so that it behoved him to have her under the same roof. She was startled to find herself being actually welcomed as a guest at the Woolpack.

Annie couldn't help being relieved. Much as she loved Dolly, it was nice to have her room to herself again, particularly as there was still so much to do. Since Aunt Jessie was at a loss to know where to find Dolly's mother, it remained for Annie to carry out the rest of the arrangements for the wedding. She ordered the catering, sent Matt to get the invitations printed with the help of a recommendation from Amos – for the invitations were to be printed at the *Hotten Courier's* works.

Faced with Joe's request, Annie made no protest. 'You'd best bed down in t'parlour,' she said. And, at the look of astonishment on her son's face at this surrender, she added hastily, 'For one night only, mind! I'm not having anyone sleep in t'parlour as a general thing.'

That evening, there was a rehearsal of the wedding ceremony. Joe was allowed to slip off early when he showed he understood his role, but Dolly and Matt were kept at the church for a long time. Afterwards Annie went for a discussion with the vicar. All in all, the family at Emmerdale were late in settling for the night, so that Matt was rather later than usual in the mistle for milking next morning.

'Afternoon,' Joe said cheerfully to him as he came in.

'Sorry I'm behind this morning. Never knew talking could make you so tired!'

'You and your cousin kept it up for a bit after I'd turned in, didn't you?'

'Oh, aye. There's such a lot to catch up with! And then Ma was wondering what to do about the day.'

'What day?'

'*The* day. Wedding day. She were saying, where's Dolly to get wed from?'

'From here, of course,' Joe said.

'Nay,' Matt protested. 'We're not supposed to see each other on t'wedding day until we meet in church.'

'Oh aye, that's right! I'd forgot that. Can't she be wed from Woolpack?'

'She could,' Matt said on a note of doubt, 'but I get the impression that Amos will send her into hysterics wi' his anxieties about his part in the wedding.'

'Well, how about Demdyke then?'

'Pip Coulter's there.'

'There's two bedrooms, Matt.'

'Aye,' Matt said, but without enthusiasm.

'What's wrong?'

'To tell the truth, Dolly got a bit weepie last night, about Pip and Steve. Said, didn't it seem wrong, that we were going to be so happy and all, while Pip and Steve were going to be just t'opposite. And you know, Joe ... it does seem sort of funny, doesn't it – that they'd be under one roof, one with such a terrible prospect ahead of her and t'other all good things?'

'That's right,' Joe said, looking sad. 'Poor little thing ... It'd be no fun for her to see Dolly putting on the glad rags and everything. Because, you know, her and Steve ...'

'Aye,' Matt said. 'You don't have to spell it out for me. She's expecting, isn't she?'

'How d'you know that?'

'Caught sight of her in Beckindale the day she came back. I knew then ... How old is she, Joe?'

'Not seventeen yet.'

'And her folks've turned her out?'

'Aye.'

'Well, you did a good thing when you took her under your wing, lad,' Matt said, with unexpected fervour. It was so rare to see Matt carried away that Joe was quite taken aback.

Just showed, didn't it, how it frayed a feller's nerves, being involved in a wedding!

Joe intended to drop in at Demdyke after the milking, just to make sure all was well with Pip. But the delivery man came with a load of calves nuts, and by the time he'd stowed that and got up to the top field to recapture a straying heifer, it was almost midday.

It was a pity he didn't get to Demdyke, for Pip Coulter had had a visitor.

Tom Hawker saw her being escorted there the previous day by Joe Sugden. He hung around to watch what came next, half-expecting Joe to fetch her parents. But Joe went away to visit the vicar, then returned only briefly to Demdyke. Tom Hawker waited and watched until it was almost closing time, then went to have a couple of quick pints in the Woolpack. As far as he could gather from the gossip there, no one knew Pip was at Demdyke; the talk was all about the rehearsal for the Skilbeck-Acaster wedding.

Hawker's thought processes were slow, but by next morning it had occurred to him that there was a way of putting most of the blame for the hold-up on to Pip Coulter. From what he could gather, her family had thrown her out. No one was going to stand up for her. If she were to be scared away, so that she didn't turn up at the trial, then Steve's lawyer could claim that Pip Coulter had led Steve on. That way, he was sure to receive a more lenient sentence.

Hawker kept watch at Demdyke next morning until from seeing Pip pass and re-pass the window, he was sure she was the only occupant of the little house. Then he went quickly to the door to knock.

As soon as Pip saw him, she tried to close the door again. He put his foot in the way. 'I want a word with you,' he said in a menacing tone.

'Go away,' she said.

'Nay, you'll not get rid of me like that. I'm coming in.'

'No –!'

'I've got summat to say to thee. Dosta want the rest of the world to hear it?'

Scared, she backed into the cottage enough to let him in. She was frightened of him both physically and emotionally. He was much bigger than she was, and there was rage glinting in his eyes – he might actually hit her. Moreover, his anger had a force that cowed her; she understood that he felt her to blame for what had happened to Steve. And she felt he was right.

'Now,' he said as soon as he was into the livingroom, 'start packing.'

'What?'

He grabbed up the tote bag which was all she'd been able to bring from home when her mother turned her out. 'Put thy things in that and get going.'

'Going? What do you mean? Where would I go?'

'That's thy business. You're going out o' Beckindale – that's all I know.'

'No, I'm not. I can't go. You don't understand –'

'I understand well enough. Thee and thy like – ! Trouble, misery – that's all. So get going. Out!'

'No –'

'You'll go,' he said. 'My lad'll have some sort of a chance in court if you're gone.'

'But I can't go –'

'Sitha,' he said, grabbing the front of her dress and dragging her close, 'I know about the baby.'

She shuddered but no words came as she stared at him in fear.

'Steve wrote to his mother. I wasn't supposed to see the letter but I got it out o' her handbag. So I know – you're expecting a brat. And my lad believe it's his.'

'It is!' she cried. 'You know it is!'

'I know nowt o't'sort! You're the kind that'd go with anybody. Don't think I didn't see you coming out of the barn with Joe Sugden last night –'

'Oh, that was – You can't think –'

'I know what it meant. Don't try and pull the wool. So get packing and get out.'

'No, don't you see, I can't –'

'You'll go,' he said, 'if you feel anything for Steve.'

'I love Steve! You know I do –'

'Do you? Eh? Love him, do you? Wouldn't want him to know the bad things you've been up to?'

'What?' she said. 'I ... I don't understand –'

'You'll go,' he said, 'or I'll tell Steve you've slept wi' Joe Sugden –'

'No, it's not true! Steve wouldn't believe you!'

'He'd believe me all right – when I tell him you're living wi' Joe Sugden in his house at Demdyke.'

Tears welled up and began to spill over on to her cheekbones. 'Oh, you wouldn't,' she said brokenly. 'You wouldn't tell a lie like that to your own son!'

'I'd do owt I could to get you out o' his life. So are you going?'

She looked at him and saw an implacable enemy. From somewhere she found a resource of calmness. She blinked back the tears.

There was nothing for it. She would have to pack and go.

CHAPTER NINE

When Joe found the house empty again at midday, his first reaction was annoyance. He wanted to help Pip, and he understood that a lass expecting a baby would be subject to emotional ups and downs. But she might have some sort of consideration for other folk.

He'd brought a pie, given him by Annie, for their meal. He'd also brought some milk and some fresh fruit, since Annie felt Pip ought to have fresh fruit in her diet. He had them in a carton in his arms. He set the carton down on the table and went up to look in the bedroom. Pip hadn't answered his call but she might be asleep on the bed.

But the room was empty. And moreover, her belongings were gone. Her toothbrush and facecloth weren't in the bathroom. And downstairs, her tote-bag wasn't hanging on the hook where she'd put it.

So she'd packed up and gone.

His first thought was, 'Silly little thing.' He stamped around the kitchen for a minute or two, feeling hard done by. Then realising he was hungry, he cut a hunk of pie and ate that. He put the kettle on for a cup of coffee.

It was then he noticed she'd not washed up her breakfast things. Now, that was odd. Last time she walked out, she'd shown some sort of gratitude by leaving everything tidy. But this time, there was a sort of haphazard look to the place. It was almost as if she'd packed up and gone all in two minutes.

Well, happen that was how it had come about. She'd had a sudden impulse and put her things in the bag and walked out.

But where to? Where the dickens did she think she was going? She'd been so thankful to have a place to lay her head.

Unless she'd heard from Steve ...? Had a message he

wanted her nearer to him so she could visit? But no, it couldn't be that. They wouldn't let her visit Steve. She was involved in the crime and surely they wouldn't allow them to confer together in case they cooked up a tale.

Nay, she hadn't gone to be near Steve. But then, why had she gone?

He drank his coffee, ate one of the apples, took another look round the house, then gave up. He had work to do. Nobody could say he hadn't tried to help her.

That evening, the village constable, P.C. Edwards, drove up to Emmerdale as Joe was finishing tea with his family. 'Could I have a word in your ear, Joe?' he inquired, and strolled with him from the farmhouse door back to his car. 'I just wanted to let you know ... Since you're standing bail for her, like ...'

'What?' Joe asked in alarm.

'Pip Coulter didn't report at the police cottage today.'

Joe met his gaze. 'Oh, heck,' he said.

'I thought I ought to just let you know. If you have any idea what she's doing, remind her she ought to have reported in. It's not too bad if she just misses one day, but if she doesn't come in tomorrow, I'll have to report back.'

'Damn and blast,' Joe said with force. He saw Edwards staring at him and went on in self-accusation: 'I should've known! She's stopping at my cottage in Demdyke but when I dropped in at lunchtime with summat for her to eat, she were gone. I should've known.'

'You mean – she's scarpered?'

'Looks like it. Her things were gone.'

Edwards' plump face shadowed. 'Hey-up, Joe! You're her surety – for five hundred quid.'

'Don't remind me. Look, Bill, she's not gone far. She ... she's not on quite an even keel so she's likely to do daft things like this. We'll find her, never fear.'

'I hope so,' Edwards said heavily. 'It's goin' to be bad if she's run right off.'

Joe hurried indoors to tell his mother. Annie immediately rang the vicar to ask his advice. Hinton was very worried at the news. 'Annie, this couldn't be worse,' he said. 'You realise that, in her condition ... ?'

'Only too well, vicar. What should we do?'

'Let's wait a bit. She may come back to the cottage to

sleep. In fact, she *must* come back, Annie. Where else can she go?'

But she didn't come back, and by next morning Mr Hinton was more alarmed than he liked to show. He remembered only too well how strangely Tom Hawker had behaved, how resentfully he had spoken of Pip. Hinton had gone through all the obvious lines of search as soon as the day was begun: tried to speak to Pip's mother and was told to clear off, tried to speak to Tom Hawker and was greeted with abuse. By and by Mrs Hawker came to see him at the vicarage, looking scared and furtive.

She was a tiny woman with a lined face. Years of coping with her ill-tempered, lazy husband had given her a sad aura. She said to Hinton: 'I don't like to think it, vicar, but I'm feared my man has done summat to that lass.'

'Done something?' Hinton repeated, looming over her with anxiety. 'What kind of something?'

'I don't know. But he was as pleased as punch with himself last night. Took a bit too much to drink and was crowing to me he'd got rid of Steve's biggest problem.'

'Got rid of – ? What d'you think that means?'

'I dunno, really, vicar,' she confessed. 'I mean, if truth's told, Tom himself is Steve's biggest problem. But he don't see it that way, of course. I thought he meant Pip Coulter.' She hesitated and went on in a faltering voice: 'Then you came this morning asking if he'd seen her.'

'But he said no, as well as I could understand him.'

'I think he were lying. I think ... if t'lass is gone ... I think he had summat to do wi' it.'

'Mrs Hawker! You don't think he'd ... harm Pip?'

She got up from the chair in which he'd put her and moved about the room, clasping and unclasping her hands. 'It's a terrible thing to say of my own man,' she admitted, 'but he's capable of hurting a lass.'

'Will you ask him whether he's seen Pip, done anything?' Hinton knew he was asking a lot, and was surprised by her reply.

'I've already done that!' she flashed. 'I charged him wi' being up to summat, the minute you'd gone. Oh, we had a real up-and-down. But I couldn't get anything out o' him and he's gone lowping off ... I don't know where he is now. All I know is, he's not ignorant of what's happened to Pip.'

After this spate of words, energy seemed to desert her. She could contribute little more. After she'd gone the vicar thought for a bit then went to the telephone. He rang Emmerdale.

'Annie,' he said, 'I've had a conversation with Mrs Hawker that's very worrying. I may be over-anxious, but ... I think we ought to get out a search party to look for Pip Coulter.'

'A search party?' Annie drew in a breath. 'You mean she may be lying somewhere? Ill? Injured?'

'Let's not go beyond this, Annie. We ought to go out and look for her rather than wait for her to come back. Will you see if your menfolk can spare time to make a search of Emmerdale land?'

'Of course they'll spare time, vicar,' she replied at once. 'And I'll ring round the other farms, shall I?'

'Would you? I'll go across to the Woolpack and see if I can enlist Henry and Amos.'

At the Woolpack Henry was searching for a saucepan in which to boil a breakfast egg. Amos was on the telephone about arrangements for the forthcoming wedding. Dolly, who had moved in the previous night, was tidying the bar. When they heard the vicar's request Dolly was the first to volunteer.

'Nay,' Henry said. 'It'd be best if you stopped here and looked after t'bar –'

'Alone?' Amos began, affronted. It was against his principles to let a female person have sole control of his bar. But at a glare from Henry he fell silent.

'We could go on and do a bit of shopping after,' Henry pointed out.

The fact was, he and Amos had agreed to club together in buying the wedding present, and wanted to get to Hotten to choose something. Here was the ideal opportunity; they could leave Dolly in charge while they did their share of looking for Pip Coulter in the barns and outhouses, and then drive straight on to Hotten.

'Quite right!' Amos said with a promptness that took Dolly by surprise. She was even quite flattered: fancy Amos allowing her free rein in his precious pub.

Spring had been late and cold that year. Now that the weather was warming up, most farmers wanted to be out on their land. Yet without hesitation they downed tools at the call to help in the search for Pip Coulter.

Joe recalled that he'd found her in the barn by the top pasture. He headed there first, but there was no sign that she'd been back. He and Matt divided the terrain between them, looking in every ditch, behind every wall, in every thicket. No results.

Meanwhile Constable Edwards tackled Tom Hawker. The vicar had said he thought Hawker was in some way responsible for her disappearance though in what way he couldn't quite explain. But Edwards was used to putting two and two together; he knew Hawker felt his son had been led astray by Pip and he guessed that Hawker had been after the lass. Perhaps he'd threatened her, or even beaten her up. So now she was hiding until she felt it was safe to come out.

Worse things than that, Edwards didn't want to consider.

But Hawker refused to co-operate. 'I've nowt to say,' he kept repeating. 'Are you charging me with summat? If so, what? Charge me, and I'll answer the charge!'

'Nay, now, Tom ... all I want is information,' the constable pleaded.

'I've nowt to say,' Hawker said.

Yet Edwards was satisfied the man knew something. He even tried keeping him under surveillance for an hour or so, but Hawker didn't do anything. He sat indoors watching the racing on television, then when Dolly Acaster opened the Woolpack, he strolled to the pub for a jar.

And you can't arrest a man for watching racing or taking a jar.

Amos and Henry did their stint of the search. They took the dykes and hedges along the main road from Beckindale to the main Bradford crossroads, faithfully scrambling behind each one and pulling back every screening branch with a walking stick. At the crossroads they reported back from the phone box: no sign of Pip Coulter.

'That's a blessing, any road,' Henry said as he got back in to drive on to Hotten.

'You mean, not to have found her?'

'Not to have found her in a ditch,' Henry retorted.

'Oh aye.' Amos stared through the windscreen. 'If you want my opinion, she's gone off to Bradford or Leeds to continue her life of crime.'

'Nay, Amos, she's nobbut a kid!'

'That kid, as you call her Mr Wilks, held up our pub at gunpoint.'

'She didn't touch the gun, Amos.'

'But she didn't prevent Steve Hawker pointing it at us, did she?'

'No, that's true. But see here ... we weren't harmed –'

'Not harmed? Shut up for hours and hours in a cold cellar? Why, we might not have been found till midday –'

'But the vicar and Mr Pangrave heard us in the early morning –'

'But they weren't to know that when they locked us in, were they?'

Henry could only agree Amos was right there. All the same, he hoped Amos wasn't going to be so unrelenting when he gave evidence in court. In Henry's opinion, those two kids had been pushed to what they did by a set of parents who ought to be made to answer for their behaviour too.

In Hotten, he and Amos got to cross purposes almost at once. Amos wished to buy a piece of silver for Dolly, but something that would be used every day so that as he said, 'she'll always remember us.' But the wife of a young farmer doesn't have much time for setting out silver. If Amos had been content with a set of serving spoons, it might have been feasible – Henry could envisage Dolly putting them on the table alongside the mashed potatoes every day. Amos, however, wanted something a bit more showy. And Henry knew from his own experience of married life that things like silver teapots weren't so much used as put up on shelves or in glass-fronted cabinets.

They went from shop to shop in Hotten – from jeweller to antique shop to curio shop to furniture shop. Nothing they saw quite fitted the bill. It had to be quite large, so as to look as if it was worth the money. And sparkly, so as to catch the eye. And useful. And in good taste. And the kind of thing Dolly would like.

They were staring in the window of a craftsman's boutique when Henry caught sight of something in a mirror on sale there.

'Hey-up, Amos, look at that!'

'What?' said Amos. 'Now, Mr Wilks, we don't want to buy a mirror –'

'Nay, Amos, in the mirror. *In* the mirror!'

112

Amos frowned, looked, and exclaimed in surprise. 'Why, it's Pip!'

'Aye.' Henry caught his arm. 'Don't look round, it might frighten her off.'

They watched the slight figure in the mirror. The view showed them the other side of the road and some way up the pavement from where they were standing. The angle at which the mirror hung in the window let them see her without being seen themselves.

'What are we going to do?' Amos said. 'We can't just stand here and let her disappear again.'

'Mmm.' Henry said, tugging at his moustache. 'I'm just thinking. That's a bus stop where she's standing, isn't it?'

'Aye,' returned Amos with some scorn, 'and if you had to manage wi'out a car as most of us do, you'd know that's the stop for the Beckindale bus.'

'Does that mean she's going back to Beckindale, then?'

'Well, here's the bus ...' The single decker red bus drew to a stop. When it moved off again, Pip was gone. 'She got on,' Amos said.

'So she's going back.'

'That don't follow, Mr Wilks. That bus stops other places afore it gets to Beckindale.'

'Where, for instance?'

'Connelton. Goes a bit roundabout. You see,' Amos said with heavy sarcasm, 'it has to take people to where they live if they've got no car, so it covers a biggish area. Pip Coulter could get off at half a dozen places along the way.'

'Where's a phone?' exclaimed Henry, turning away in haste.

'Hang on, Mr Wilks –'

'Can't stop, Amos. I've got to let 'em know in Beckindale, so's she can be met off the bus.'

'Oh, ah! So now you agree wi' me she has to be taken into custody –'

'Not a bit. She's got to be met so she can't be scared by Tom Hawker again.'

That gentleman was sitting morosely in the Woolpack, well into his third pint and feeling put upon. Dolly Acaster was serving alone in the bar, which wasn't very busy, and she was whispering with those toffee-nosed new relations of Matt Skilbeck's. Hawker was sure they were whispering about

113

him. As it happened, for once he was right.

'They neither of them had a very happy life,' Dolly was murmuring to Polly Ferris, speaking of Pip and Steve. 'Mr Pearson was just saying the other evening that Steve's father had always had a reputation for being hard to handle. He seems to have been very heavy-handed in dealing with the lad. And as to Pip's parents ... her mother, any road ...' Dolly cast her eyes up. 'She's impossible.'

'Well, when we passed Joe on the road a bit back, he said there'd been no sign of the girl,' Alec Ferris reported. 'He seemed genuinely upset.'

'Oh aye. He's fond of her. Used to let her ride on his handlebars when she was a kiddie.' Dolly leaned closer. 'That's the boy's father over there.'

Polly Ferris let her dark eyes rest on the man's back. 'He doesn't look a very savoury character.'

'I don't know him myself,' Dolly admitted. 'But Annie doesn't seem to have much time for him – and that's saying something.'

The door to the street opened. Mrs Hawker came in, a cardigan pulled over her house frock. She looked almost haggard with worry. Yet with a strange kind of courage she walked up to the big man who was her husband.

'Tom.'

He half-turned in his chair. He glowered. 'What you want in here?' he demanded. In his opinion, decent women didn't come into pubs.

'You know what I want, Tom. I want you to say what you did to Pip Coulter.'

'Gerroff! I didn't do owt to her.'

'Then you said summat. You told me you –'

'I told you nothing. Shut your mouth!'

'Tom, that lass is with child, and it's our Steve's babby –'

'I told you, gerroff, didn't I?'

'Tom, the babby's our flesh and blood –'

'Thassa tale,' Hawker burst in drunkenly. 'Just summat she told him to make him go off wi' her! That's the truth, for she told me so herself!'

'Ah!' cried Betty Hawker. 'You swore to me you hadn't seen her!'

'No more I had,' he growled, trying to retrieve his mistake, 'not yesterday ... But when she first come back ... I faced

114

her out ... And you want to know what she tol' me? You want to know who her kid's Dad is? Then I'll tell you. I'll tell you!'

'It's Steve, Tom. Our Steve.'

'No it isn't. She said to me. The baby's Joe Sugden's.' He swung round to glare at the group by the bar. 'And you can tell 'em that up at Emmerdale!'

Dolly went red with anger at the attack. Matt's cousin looked astounded, turned to her husband for reassurance. But next moment their attention was diverted from Hawker. The door of the pub had already been swinging as he spoke.

Joe Sugden was on the threshold.

'Joe ...' gasped Dolly.

Unheeding, Joe stepped forward. Something about him made Hawker stumble to his feet. He knew he should escape.

As he rose, Joe swung. He had a moment's intense satisfaction as his fist made contact. He hit the exact centre of Tom Hawker's lantern jaw.

And Tom Hawker went flying over backwards.

CHAPTER TEN

Betty Hawker helped her husband to his feet. Scared and shaken, he squirmed out of her grasp. In a moment he was off, out the door.

Everyone was staring at Joe. He was still angry, but embarrassed. 'I'm sorry, Mrs Hawker,' he grunted, 'but I couldn't let him say that.'

'Don't apologise, Joe,' Betty Hawker said with a sigh. 'It's what he needed!'

'Look, it's true I've been around Pip – I found her a place to sleep because she was kipping in one of our barns. Happen your husband saw me coming out of the barn with her at nightfall –'

'It's all right, Joe –'

'And I took her to Demdyke. But I've slept at the farm.' Joe was intent on making her understand. It was outrageous to him that anyone should think he'd lay a finger on Pip. She was like a kid sister to him.

'I know, lad,' Mrs Hawker agreed. 'So does everyone. So does *he*.' A jerk of her head to the door through which her husband scuttled made it clear whom she meant. 'But to get at Steve he'll say anything.'

'To get at Steve?' Joe exclaimed. 'I thought it were Pip he were getting at?'

'Nay, Joe, he wants to hurt Pip 'cos he knows it'll hurt Steve. The lad's nearly out of his mind, stuck there in prison, wondering what's happening to his girl. He feels right responsible – it's his child, Pip's his girl, he *wants* to do what he should ... So Tom knows the lad'll suffer if Pip suffers. And what Tom wants is to do him down.'

'But that's his own son –'

Betty shook her head. 'I can't explain it. He's always hated Steve. But then,' she sighed, 'he doesn't like anybody, really.'

116

Polly Ferris came forward to begin putting the room straight. 'That was quite like a film!' she remarked.

'Aye,' Joe agreed. 'But what they don't show in films is how it hurts you!' He nursed his right hand, which had come in contact so satisfyingly with Hawker's chin. 'I think I've busted it!'

Dolly touched his shoulder. 'You've busted the chair,' she told him, pointing.

True enough – the chair Tom Hawker had been sitting on was in pieces – its back had parted from the seat.

'I never did that!'

'He did it, from you hitting him. Amos isn't going to like that,' mourned Dolly.

Joe knew that was only too true. He was pretty sure he'd end up paying for the chair – but even that wouldn't really satisfy Amos.

'Tell me,' Alec Ferris inquired, 'does this sort of thing happen often in Yorkshire villages? I always thought of them as quiet places.'

'It's never happened to *me* before,' Joe confessed. 'And I'm not keen for it to happen again.' His right hand was throbbing and aching painfully. I just lost my temper.'

'Not surprising,' Alec said. 'I know the feeling.'

'Do you?' his wife put in. 'When counsel baits you in court, you never lose your temper. You stay icy cool.'

'In court? What court's that?' Joe said, advancing to the bar. 'I'll have a pint, Dolly, to help me recover.'

'You need a bandage on that,' she suggested, touching the graze on his knuckles. When he winced she said, 'And padding.'

'I'll get Ma to tie it up for me.'

'What on earth is she going to say when you tell her you hit Tom Hawker?'

'She'll say, "Jolly good!"' Alec suggested. 'No, let me pay for this, Joe.'

Joe raised his eyebrows. 'Approve, do you?'

'I just think it's good to see someone with the courage to do what I'd be too cagey to do.'

'Let's call it "well-informed", dear,' his wife put in. 'You'd be remembering that Tom Hawker could bring a suit for assault.'

'Ah,' Joe said, taking the jar from Dolly with thankfulness, 'you're summat to do with the law, then? In court, you said.'

'I'm a barrister.'

'Barrister? That's sort of high-powered, isn't it?'

'Well, no, there are some very low-powered barristers,' Alec laughed.

'Wait, though – Henry's been saying all along he knew your face. Seen it in t'papers, has he? Are you a famous Q.C.?'

'I'm a Q.C.,' Alec agreed.

'Wow ...' breathed Dolly.

'You are, are you,' Joe mused, drinking again. 'Listen, what's the position on Pip and Steve, then? I mean ... they're both minors, viewed by the law. But after all, fair's fair – she's having a baby and he's the father and they have a right to say what ought to happen about that, haven't they? You can see their folk aren't going to be much help –'

'I can't do anything about that, Joe. They both have legal representation.'

'You mean it's like doctors. You can't interfere?'

Alec was saved from a reply by the sudden eruption of Joe's grandfather into the pub. 'Dolly!' he cried, out of breath. 'Dolly!'

'Eh? What?' said Dolly, looking past the group at the bar.

'Dolly, your mother's back!'

'Back? Back where?'

'Here! In Beckindale.'

'Are you sure?' Dolly gasped, relieved that at last this elusive parent had turned up.

'I've just been talking to her! And Dolly – she's not alone!'

'What?' Dolly said. 'How d'you mean?'

'She's ... er ... not alone ... Joe, she stopped me in the High Street and asked me for the key of Demdyke.'

Joe stared at his grandfather over his glass. 'She what?'

'So I gave it to her.'

'You didn't!'

'I did! Joe, you don't refuse things to that woman!'

'Now look here, Grandad – there's only two bedrooms at Demdyke and Dolly's to have one so as to be married from there, and t'other's for Pip when she comes back.'

'If she comes back,' Polly Ferris put in.

'When she comes back,' Sam corrected her. 'She's arrived. I saw her getting off t'bus.'

'Pip Coulter?'

'Aye. I were going to take t'bus – to go to Ingleton for a special reason of mine ... that's why I was in t'High Street when your mother turned up, Dolly. And I missed the bus because she detained me, talking.'

'I'm sorry, Mr Pearson, but at least we know she's here, safe and sound.'

'Aye, she's here,' Sam agreed, but looking dubious.

'But she can't put up at Demdyke,' Joe insisted. 'There's no room, if Pip's back. There's no room for one, let alone her and a friend.'

'I ... er ... think it's rather more than a friend,' Sam faltered.

'You mean she's brought Aunt Jessie,' Dolly said.

'Nay, lass. It's a man.'

'A man?' Dolly looked at him in consternation.

There was a silence in the Woolpack. Alec and Polly Ferris could see something very unusual was happening which touched their cousin's bride-to-be. Old Walter, safe in his corner of the bar with his pint, was delighted by this free entertainment. Joe and Dolly waited with baited breath for Sam to continue.

'She says he's her husband,' Sam said.

'*What?*' cried Dolly.

'And what's more, her and her husband are moving into Demdyke so she can direct your wedding!'

Dolly made as if she would immediately rush from the Woolpack in search of her mother. But second thoughts restrained her. She was here to look after the bar until Mr Brearley or Mr Wilks returned. She sank against the wood counter, eyes wide. 'You've made a mistake, Mr Pearson,' she whispered.

'Nay, lass. She introduced him: "My husband, Leonard Purwick".'

'Purwick? I've never heard of him! Oh, dear heaven, what's she done?'

Joe put down his empty glass. 'I'll go, shall I?' he suggested. 'If Pip's back, as Grandad says – I ought to see if I can get in touch and take her back to Demdyke.'

'When you get there, if my mother's there ... Joe ... tell her to stop there. I need to talk to her.'

'Will do,' Joe said, and went out.

He hurried to his little house in Demdyke Row. At that

moment Annie was escorting Pip into the police house to the north of the village.

Pip had been surprised to see her, but for Annie the meeting was exactly what she'd expected. The phone call from Henry in Hotten had alerted her; she was sure Pip was coming back to report to the constable as was required by the terms of her bail. Annie knew that Pip was fond of Joe, who had stood surety. She wouldn't let him down if she could possibly help it.

'Constable Edwards is expecting you,' Annie told her as Pip joined her at the gate.

'Missed me, has he?' Pip asked with some bitterness.

'You've no idea how many people have been out looking for you.' And as Pip turned a startled face towards her, Annie added quickly, 'Not to catch you – no, not that. But worried about you, and not wanting you to miss reporting. For that'd mean going back to jail till the trial, wouldn't it?'

'If they'd found me,' Pip challenged. 'It was more so that Joe wouldn't have to pay out all that money – that's why I'm back.'

'Why did you run away in t'first place?'

Pip shivered. She was very pale and worn. Her dark eyes looked huge in her piquant face. 'I was told Joe would ... be involved ...'

'But he is involved, lass.'

'Yes, but in a different way. Oh, I don't want to talk about it.'

'Well, let's get in and see Mr Edwards,' Annie said with briskness to do away with the distress in Pip's face. 'Then I'll take you back to Demdyke.'

The interview with the constable was short and businesslike. He asked with some sternness why she hadn't reported yesterday; she replied that someone had frightened her into leaving Beckindale. Edwards studied her before inquiring the culprit. She hung her head but under pressure finally muttered: 'Mr Hawker.'

'Hm ...' said Edwards. 'I thought as much.'

'Don't put anything down on your reports about him,' Pip begged. 'Things are bad enough as it is.'

'Well, as to that ...'

'Please, Mr Edwards! I've come back, haven't it? I don't want to drag him in.'

'We'll see,' the constable said. Privately he was longing for a chance to get Tom Hawker in front of the magistrates for a hefty fine. Of all the malicious, obstructive beings in Beckindale, Hawker was one of the worst. But so far there had never been any actual evidence that would stand up in court, and Edwards had a feeling that this was another example of the same. This poor little lass had troubles enough without involving her in charging Tom Hawker with threatening behaviour.

When the report was settled and Pip had signed the attendance list, Annie took her out. 'We'll get you to Demdyke and make you a cup of tea,' she said.

But she was totally mistaken. When they arrived, they found Joe standing in consternation in the middle of the living room as Mrs Acaster unpacked a case of provisions. 'There, Leonard dear, put that in the sideboard,' she commanded. 'We'll want to offer a glass of sherry to guests before and after t'wedding.'

'Mrs Acaster!' gasped Annie.

'How are you, Mrs Sugden?' Beaming, Mrs Acaster surged forward. 'I want you to meet my husband, Leonard. Leonard, this is Mrs Sugden, who's by way of a mother to our Dolly's bridegroom Matt.'

'How d'ye do?' said Leonard. He was a man of small stature as to height, but had some girth. His face was round and rosy. He reminded Annie of illustrations she'd seen in volumes of Dickens; he was Mr Pickwick to the life.

'You're a sort of relation by marriage to Matt,' he was saying. 'Same here – I'm a sort of relation by marriage to Dolly.'

'You're her father now, Leonard,' Mrs Acaster said fondly.

'But Mrs Acaster –'

'I'm Mrs Purwick now,' Dolly's mother pointed out. 'We were married yesterday.'

'Yesterday?'

Annie had her arm protectively around Pip when they arrived. She was now clutching the girl as if she were the only reality in a nightmare. She looked at Joe. Joe raised his eyebrows and spread his hands. Having done so, he winced and put his right hand under his left arm, as if to nurse it. Annie watched him in bewilderment – you'd almost say Joe had bruised his knuckles in a prizefight. But that was just one more impossibility in a whole catalogue of impossibilities.

'Does ... does Dolly know?' Annie asked.

'Oh, I expect so,' said Dolly's mother with total blitheness. 'We spoke to your father in the High Street and then afterwards he went into the Woolpack. So I expect he told her.'

'You mean you let her find out that way? Didn't you write? Send a wire?'

'What was the need for that, Mrs Sugden? When we were coming here to take charge of the wedding? Leonard wanted us to go to the West Indies for our honeymoon, but I said, "No, Leonard, we owe it to our Dolly to see her through her wedding before we begin to savour the delights of a honeymoon." So we went to Scarborough. Just for the one night.'

The sudden descent from the poetry of the West Indies to the practicality of Scarborough in a late cold spring suddenly roused Annie to an understanding of what was happening. 'Mrs Acaster – I mean Purwick ... You can't take charge of the wedding now. Things are more or less settled –'

'Nonsense, there's still masses to do, I'm sure. As to the wedding gown –'

'It's made!' cried Annie. 'Oyster satin brocade, twelve yards of it. Aunt Jessie paid.'

'Ah yes, Jessie will be here today too,' said Phyllis Acaster, now Purwick. 'She'll share that other bedroom with Dolly.'

'But –' began both Annie and Joe, looking protectively at Pip.

'Never mind,' Annie went on, taking Pip by the arm. 'You're to come to Emmerdale.'

'Oh, Mrs Sugden, I couldn't – I'm such a nuisance when you've got so much to think on –'

'Nay, now, lass, you're coming with me.' Annie led her out. 'I'll see you later, Mrs Ac – I mean, Purwick.'

'Call me Phyllis,' she replied, seeing them out as if she owned the place. 'And you must call Leonard by his first name too. After all, we're to be related, aren't we?'

'Yes,' Annie agreed faintly, and left.

On the pavement Joe gave a sudden confused grin. 'Bye!' he remarked. 'Alec was asking if Yorkshire villages were usually so full o' action and I told him they weren't. Happen I was wrong!'

'I could do with a bit less,' his mother rejoined. 'But we'll sort it. Dolly does know?'

'Aye, Grandad came gasping in with the news. She's coming here as soon as Amos or Henry gets back. Oh,' groaned Joe as he remembered, 'goodness knows what Amos will say about that chair!'

'What chair?'

'A chair got broken. Ma, can I follow you up to Emmerdale to get a bandage round this hand?'

'What did you do to it?'

'I collided with something. See you in a minute, eh? And you'd best tell Matt what's happened.'

His mother suddenly realised that this was why Joe wanted her to reach the farm ahead of him. Someone had to tell Matt that his bride's mother had reappeared, not only by herself causing confusion but bringing with her a new husband. Sighing, Annie put Pip in her car and drove home.

Dolly locked up the Woolpack at the end of the midday opening. She hadn't waited to wash up the glasses or tidy the place. Her whole attention was on the matter of getting to Demdyke and seeing this gigolo her mother had married.

Yet why should it be a gigolo? Men like that went for older women with money, and her mother didn't have much. Still, there were men who battened on lonely widows, happy to find someone who'd do their washing and cook their meals and run round after them.

She hurried to Demdyke but her steps slowed as she came up the path. How did you greet a newly-married mother? How did you speak to a newly-acquired father?

The door swung open before she could knock. 'Ah, my Dorothy!' cried Phyllis Purwick, enfolding her in her arms. 'Isn't this a lovely surprise?' She led her indoors. 'This is my little girl, Leonard. Isn't she lovely?'

Leonard had risen from his knees; he was apparently stocking the sideboard with wine bottles. He held out his hand. 'Pleased to meet you,' he said.

'Mother, would you please tell me what you are up to?' Dolly burst out almost fiercely.

Phyllis raised her eyebrows. 'Well, I'm married, dear, of course. Didn't Mr Pearson tell you? Leonard is your new father.'

'Pleased and proud,' put in Leonard, beaming.

He certainly looked less like a gigolo than any man Dolly could imagine. Round and cuddly, he looked as if he only needed a Father Christmas outfit to be distributing presents. He had been busy about his chores when she came in; it dawned on her that far from taking on her mother so as to be looked after, Leonard was doing the looking-after. Moreover, he didn't seem in need of anyone else's small income; his suit was good, he smelt of good soap and cigars, he had a Seiko watch on his wrist.

'So we've come, dear, to wind up all the problems about your marriage. I know your Aunt Jessie has coped as well as she could, but there are finishing touches only a mother can give –'

'Finishing touches!' cried Dolly. 'I haven't been able to get a word out of you for weeks, you disappear without trace, and now you turn up like this when everything is fixed –'

'Nothing is fixed, Dorothy, without my approval –'

'We managed up to now without that! I'd no idea whether you were going to show up at all –'

'Dorothy,' said her mother, hurt, 'you must have known I wouldn't miss your wedding. And now of course here's Leonard, looking forward to it so much. It will be such a thrill for him to give you away.'

'Give me away?' Dolly repeated. 'Who says he's giving me away?'

'But he has to, dear. Who else? He's your father!'

Dolly looked at Leonard. He, embarrassed, gave her a self-conscious smile. They were total strangers to each other. But he was her 'father' ...

What was Amos going to say to this?

Amos and Henry returned from their gift-buying in Hotten to find the Woolpack well and truly locked. Henry amused himself by telling Amos he could sense intruders, so that Amos charged in looking like an armoured car with its gun trained. But his bellicosity ebbed away as he gazed about.

'Who did that?' he gasped.

'What?'

'That!' Amos picked up the broken chair, the back in one hand and the seat and legs in the other. 'I've never had a broken chair in any house of mine!' he cried with indignation. 'Never had breakages to write off! Somebody's ill-treated this, that's what's happened! I'll speak to Dolly very strong about this –'

'Hey, Amos,' Henry said, perplexed, 'glasses ain't been cleaned.'

Amos put down the pieces of chair. He turned his attention to the bar. 'Dirty glasses?' he whispered, disbelief in every line of his whiskered face.

'That's odd. Not like Dolly to be slack,' Henry said.

'Odd? It's monstrous! You see what I've always said? Female persons aren't fit to be left in charge –'

'There'll be a reason, Amos,' soothed Henry. 'Dolly wouldn't –'

'It's all this wedding business,' Amos said. Almost he regretted his own role in the wedding. If he weren't giving the bride away, he could disapprove whole-heartedly of any slackness brought on by the wedding. But even the wedding didn't account for the broken chair. He eyed it with incredulity.

The phone rang. Amos was still deep in thought. Henry answered.

' 'Lo?' said Matt. 'That you, Henry? Is Dolly still there, or has she gone to Demdyke?'

'She's gone, Matt. We've just got in and found the place in a bit of a pickle –'

'How d'you mean, pickle? Not been done again, have you?'

'No, no, nowt like that. Only looks as if Dolly didn't tidy up as she ought to, before she left.'

'Well, Henry, you see,' said Matt, hesitating. 'She ... er ... would be a bit put out when she left.'

'Put out? What about?'

'Well, to tell t'truth ... There's been a bit of an event.'

'What sort of event?'

'Mrs Acaster's come back.'

'But that's good.'

'Aye, in a way. Only, you see, Henry ... Annie tells me she's at Demdyke ... wi' a new husband.'

'Who?'

'Mrs Acaster.'

'At Demdyke?'

'Aye. She's Mrs Purwick now. Got wed yesterday.'

'You're joking!'

'I wish I were!' Then Matt corrected himself, 'No, of course, I don't mean that, I hope she'll be very happy an' all, but y'see, Dolly didn't know, and she's just gone to Demdyke to meet him.'

'Meet him?'

'Aye, her new father.'

'Oh, God,' groaned Henry. Terrible vistas were opening before him.

'I wanted to get a word wi' Dolly before she set out –'

'I can see your point, Matt.'

'She's gone, eh?'

' 'Fraid so.'

'Oh well ...' Henry could fancy Matt shaking his head hopelessly at the telephone. 'By the way, Henry, Annie says to thank you for the tip about Pip Coulter. She came off the bus like you said. She's here now.'

'At Emmerdale?'

'Well, yes ... Mrs Ac – Purwick and her husband have taken over at Demdyke.'

'Oh, lord,' groaned Henry.

'Henry, don't keep groaning.'

'All right, I won't,' groaned Henry, and hung up.

When he turned, Amos was regarding him severely. 'Well?' he demanded. 'That was Matt, eh? Is Dolly with him?'

'Nay, she's at Demdyke. Amos, would you like a drink?'

'Mr Wilks, what has happened to Dolly? Why did she leave the place in such a state? I am after all giving her away which gives me a special relationship.'

Henry didn't reply. He was nerving himself for the news he had to break. He went to the dispenser and got himself a whisky.

'Matt says she's had to hurry off to Demdyke to be with her mother and father. He's been trying to get hold of her –'

'No doubt, because she's no right to be out of t'Woolpack until she'd cleared up. And did he know owt about that broken chair?' Amos was stooping to examine the pieces when a thought struck him. He straightened and turned to look at Henry. 'Did you say "mother and *father*"?'

'Aye, I did,' Henry replied. He put a glass against the whisky dispenser. 'Sure you won't have a drop too?'

'Father'? Amos felt himself go cold. A great opportunity was slipping away from him.

CHAPTER ELEVEN

When Betty Hawker got home, she found her husband sitting in their kitchen-living room with a wet cloth pressed to his swollen lip.

'Where've you been?' he demanded in a muffled voice.

'In t'phone box –'

'Ringing t'police, I hope,' he snarled. 'I'll have the law on Joe Sugden –'

'The law? What for?'

'Assault and battery, that's what! I'll –'

'Tom,' said Mrs Hawker with unwonted sharpness, 'if you take Joe Sugden to court, I'll stand up and tell them that you provoked him by telling totally unfounded lies about him that you *knew* to be lies –'

'Eh?'

'And so will all the other folk that were in the bar. It'll probably end with Joe leaving without a stain on his character and you being charged by him with slander.'

'You'll say not a word except what I tell you –'

'Nay, Tom, I'll tell t'truth. And when our Steve is had up, I'm going to get in t'witness box and tell t'judge how you've always bullied and mistreated him since he were a little lad. I'll tell how you pocketed every little bit o' cash he made with part-time jobs to put on your stupid horses. I'll tell how you sold the bike Norah and Don gave him when he was fourteen, and lost it all on a cert in the Derby. I'll show them why our Steve knew it were no use turning to us for help and support when his lass told him she were expecting his babby –'

'Have you taken leave o' your senses?' Hawker cried, aghast. 'I brought up Steve to respect authority –'

'No you didn't!' she broke in. In her brown housework overall she looked like an angry little wren. It was so unusual for her to stand up to him that he couldn't believe his ears.

'You've always disliked Steve,' she went on before he could collect himself to speak. 'Ever since he were a bairn, when he got the whooping cough so bad and needed so much nursing. You hated him for waking you up at nights with his coughing. And you hated it when he started to have a bit of personality – and he wasn't a bit like you. I don't understand how a father could be so agin his own child, but that's how it's been.'

'Rubbish! Everybody in Beckindale knows I tried to bring that lad up as –'

'Folk in Beckindale aren't as thick as you think, Tom Hawker!' she flashed. 'They see you toddling to the Social Security to get your money, and then to the betting shop to get rid of it! All you wanted from Steve was that he should get a job, and keep it, so you could grab his wages for yourself. Ah, when I think how I let you –'

'Let me?'

'He was scared of you and disappointed in me. What kind of a mother have I been to the lad? I blame myself, too – not just you, Tom.'

'Steve's the one to blame! He was the one who stole a gun and held up them two in t'Woolpack –'

'Aye, but would he ever have done it if he could have come to us? He wanted to get money so him and the lass could go off, be together, get wed. And now you – you, his own dad – you're trying to drive the girl away, you're trying to separate them because you know she's all he's got! I look at you, Tom, and I wonder how any man could be so cruel.'

'I'm thinking of his good. That lass is a slut –'

'If any harm's come to her through you, Tom, I'll never forgive you!' she said. 'I looked at you today in t'Woolpack when you were scrambling away from Joe Sugden, and I suddenly saw what you really are. You're a nothing, bolstering yourself up by speaking harm of others. Well, I'm not going to help bolster you up any more. I'm leaving.'

Hawker sprang up, dropping the wet cloth and leaping towards her to grab and shake her. 'Leaving?' he said, in fury. 'What d'you mean, leaving?'

'I'm packing up and going. And don't thee try violence, Tom. If I have a bruise or a cut, Norah will be witness when I charge you with it.'

'Norah! So that's what it is! You think to go and stay wi' Norah for a bit –'

'Nay, for good, Tom. Norah and Don have been on at me often enough to move in wi' them. I rang her just gone, and she urged me to get straight on the bus wi'out even coming home to tell thee. But I wanted thee to know. It's over, Tom. You'll have no one. And you brought it on yourself.'

Her courage in the face of his physical weight made him pause. He said in scorn, 'If you think I'll let you out that door, you're daft.'

'What are you going to do? Stand guard over me? Nay, you'd get fed up of that. You'd want to get to t'betting shop in Hotten, or you'd drop off over a bottle beer. And I'd be off first chance, Tom Hawker. So don't *thee* be daft.'

She walked past him, tiny against his cadaverous length. As she reached the foot of the stairs she said, 'I'll just be packing a few things for now. Don will come for the rest in a day or two.'

There was so much certainty in the simple words that all at once he understood she meant it. All the bravado went out of him. He said, on a wheedling note, 'Now come on, Betty. You don't really mean this. We've been wed a long time. You can't just walk out.'

She didn't even bother to reply. She walked up the stairs, and in a moment he could hear drawers open and close as she collected overnight things.

He followed her up. At the room door he began, 'Betty, I never harmed the lass. I didn't lay a finger on her. She packed up and left when I told her she wasn't welcome, that's all.'

'And where was she supposed to go?'

'How do I know? She's got friends, I suppose. She got on the Hotten bus.'

'Happen I'll see her there, then,' Betty said, and snapping shut her small case, she walked by, down the stairs, out of the kitchen, and out of the house.

She had time before the bus to pass on the information about Pip. She walked to the vicarage, thinking that to inform Mr Hinton was the best plan. There, to her astonishment, she found Pip Coulter herself.

There had been a long consultation at Emmerdale over what could be done about Pip. The vicar had been summoned by telephone. The farmhouse kitchen had seemed very full, for Dolly had arrived to explain to Matt about her new stepfather.

'You'd best settle down in t'parlour,' Annie said to Pip. 'I'll bring you a pot of tea and a bit to eat, and happen you'll have a bit of a snooze afterwards, eh? The sofa's quite comfy. Meanwhile the vicar and I'll have a chat to think where you could stay for a bit.'

Annie was hoping that Mr Hinton would take Pip in. It wouldn't be impossible to find some other older female to stay at the vicarage as chaperone. It could only be a very temporary measure because it seemed likely Tom Hawker would stir up trouble about it, no matter how respectable the set-up. And there was Mr Hinton himself to consider. He would want to do his duty, but the fact remained that he was a solitary man who didn't really want lodgers – let alone young pregnant girls in trouble with the police.

Alec and Polly Ferris took part in the debate in the kitchen. Now that Joe had explained Alec's calling, it seemed natural to ask his opinion.

'Can't a room be rented for her?' Polly Ferris inquired.

Annie shook her head. 'There's not many folks around here will let rooms to a lass expecting a bairn – especially when there's no father around.'

'She shouldn't be on her own anyway,' Dolly said. 'Not how she is ...'

'You're quite right, she shouldn't,' the vicar agreed. 'And she's after all only sixteen. She needs an older person around.'

'But it's her parents' place to care for her,' Alec said. 'Are you telling me there's absolutely no chance of their rallying round?'

'You'd not ask if you knew them, Alec,' Annie sighed.

'In any case, Pip would be very unhappy if she had to go there,' the vicar put in, with memories of her desperation when she came to him, weeks ago, begging him to let her rent a room at the vicarage. How he wished now that he had agreed! No matter what the difficulties, he should have taken her in. But he had shied away from the legal embargo and the problems with her parents.

'There's one thing I'd like to point out,' Alec put in with some crispness. 'There is the very real possibility she may have to go to prison. Complicity in armed robbery is not a crime the law treats lightly.'

Dolly took Matt's hand more tightly in hers. 'It's so unfair!' she murmured. 'Why should life be so hard on Pip? I don't brush away what she did – it was wrong, I know, very wrong. But it almost seems as if her and Steve were pushed into it by their parents. Why should those two be so unhappy? I mean, when I compare Matt and me ...'

Matt smiled at her in comfort. 'We had our ups and downs too, love. But I know what you mean. We seem to have everything, really. Those two have nowt.'

'Aye, that's what I mean,' Dolly urged. 'Why is life so lucky for some and unlucky for others?'

All eyes were turned to Mr Hinton. He shook his head. 'I can't account for it,' he said. 'I could just say, it's God's will – and then you'd ask me why God should be so hard on Pip and Steve. All I can say is this: those two really love one another. If by some chance they can get through the next few weeks ... if Steve doesn't get sent away for years ... if they can just have something to look forward to, the chance to be together by and by ... those two will have more than either of their sets of parents. They'll have their love. Perhaps that's compensation for what they've gone through. Perhaps they'll have learned something that Tom Hawker and Mrs Coulter are incapable of learning.'

There was a tiny silence. Then Annie said, 'If the judge and jury could only know what those parents have been like ...'

'Huh!' said Joe.

'Well, we all know that those two aren't criminals. They're a couple of youngsters driven to do something quite out of keeping with their usual nature by the stupidity of their parents.'

'Mrs Hawker's not so bad,' Matt objected.

'She's a good body, under the thumb of a bad man. Trouble is, she was brought up to believe that the man is the head of the family so Tom's had his way. And I daresay it's hard for any woman to believe her husband really means harm to his own bairn. But that's the fact – Tom Hawker has actually been doing all he can for years to make life impossible for that lad.'

'Well,' said Alec Ferris with admiration, 'I don't think I'd mind being in the dock if I had you to defend me!'

Annie turned on him. This was far too serious for idle compliments. She'd spoken with burning conviction, and her tone was still strong as she went on: 'I'd be in the court defending Pip and Steve if I had the chance. And let me tell you, that's another of their troubles. They're getting no help defending themselves.'

'But they have legal aid,' Alec protested.

'Oh aye!' Annie brushed that away. 'But there's no one interested in them *personally*. And Steve's never been one to express himself well. I doubt if he's been able to tell his lawyer what he was up to over that gun. What's to be said in court about it then? That he stole it wi' desperate ideas of robbing a bank and settled for t'Woolpack because he were in a hurry?'

'But you have to admit, Ma,' Joe put in, 'he did saw off the barrel −'

'To hide it under his coat on t'way to t'Woolpack.' Annie threw out her hands. 'You can't tell me he did that with a view to making t'gun a more effective weapon. I know Steve Hawker. I don't believe he meant real harm to anyone. But who's to say that for him when he can't say it for himself? The jury'll hear the case and think, "Oh, another couple o' youngsters who've got to be punished for doing summat wrong." But the true fact is, they'd been punished by their parents for years before they broke out into wrongdoing.'

Polly Ferris looked at her husband. 'Can you hear the thump of a falling gauntlet?' she inquired.

Alec frowned and pushed his mug of coffee about on the wooden table. 'I know you think legal etiquette is a lot of nonsense,' he muttered, 'but I can't just walk into the office of his counsel and say, "I'm going to take over". I have to be invited in. Someone has to give me instructions.'

'Pip could retain you, couldn't she?' Hinton suggested.

'It's not Pip who needs me,' Alec said. 'With any kind of luck, Pip's counsel ought to get probation for her. But Steve will be regarded as ringleader. He's older than Pip, he led her into the crime even if she didn't actually handle the gun, he's the father of her illegitimate child. Taken at face value the case against him is bad.'

'Could Steve ask for you?'

'Steve has never even heard of me.' Alec thought about it. 'His parents could ask for my services ...'

'Huh,' Joe said again. 'Can't imagine Tom Hawker moving a finger.'

'Mrs Hawker might, though,' Annie said. 'She has been trying to get some sense out of him over Pip –'

'Aye, she'd come after him to t'Woolpack,' Joe reported.

'But she'd be too scared of him to go against him to this extent,' Matt said.

They were at an impasse. Alec said, 'Well, leave it for the moment. The prime object is to think of a place where Pip can stay.'

Hinton rose. 'It's quite clear she must come to the vicarage,' he said. 'I don't know why I've hesitated – it's most unChristian! But someone else must come as a resident, Annie. Otherwise it would be most improper.'

'Aunt Jessie!' cried Dolly. 'She's due any minute!'

Hinton smiled suddenly. Of all the elderly ladies he'd met in and around Beckindale, Aunt Jessie was one for whom he had a great deal of respect. 'Well, if you think she'd agree? The vicarage isn't really equipped for guests, as you know, Dolly. But as a temporary measure?'

Thus settled, the matter began to seem less intractable. Pip was asked if she'd like to stay at the vicarage and even her reluctance didn't seem too disappointing. Joe drove them back, trying to encourage her to think of Hinton as a friend. But she couldn't help remembering how she'd turned to him for help and how he had failed her.

But what else was she to do? She had no home, and she had to be somewhere in or near Beckindale to report daily to the police over her bail. If the vicar would take her in, she ought to be grateful.

She was upstairs looking at the sparsely furnished bedrooms when Mrs Hawker arrived. She came downstairs on hearing her voice, imagining she had news of Steve.

'Eh, lass!' Betty Hawker cried. 'I thought you were missing?'

'No, Mrs Hawker, I'm found,' Pip said with wry humour. 'Is anything wrong? Over Steve, I mean?'

'Not more than it was,' Betty sighed. 'Nay, I came on purpose to tell you, Mr Hinton, that Tom had admitted herding t'lass out of Beckindale. But it seems she's herded herself back!'

'You've actually been able to get information like that from your husband?' Hinton said in surprise.

'You may well remark on it,' Betty said. 'I should've stood

up to him years gone. But better late than never.' She indicated the small case at her feet. 'I've left him, vicar.'

'Oh, Mrs Hawker – !'

'I know you probably don't agree with it, but –'

'No, there are circumstances, Mrs Hawker,' he hastened to assure her. 'The church does not require anyone to be victimised in matrimony. Come inside – we have a lot to talk about.'

She had thought to catch the afternoon bus but now realised she wouldn't make it. But it was more important to speak to the vicar and Steve's lass. She'd always liked what she knew of Pip – a shy, quiet girl, kept under far too strict a control by her mother.

She explained to Mr Hinton that her cousin in Hotten would give her a room. 'She's been at me for years to go and live there,' she explained. 'They have a great old house on the cliff by the river – you know that road? Don's a builder and decorator, does well. They've plenty of room there so I don't feel I'm being a burden.'

'Hm.' said Hinton. 'Pip is staying with me for the present...'

'Oh aye, you've plenty of room here,' Mrs Hawker began, then broke off. 'Not alone?' she asked.

'No, Miss Acaster's aunt is coming, I believe –'

'Good gracious, what a dealing and doiling! Wouldn't it be better if Pip came along of me? My cousin Norah would take us both, I'm sure.'

Hope leaped in Pip's eyes. To be with 'real' people – not a vicar and an old lady ... But then she remembered her situation and said, 'You can't be sure she'd want me. I mean ... there's the baby coming and everything.'

'I'll ring Norah and ask her this minute, if you like,' Mrs Hawker replied. 'If I could use your phone, vicar?'

'Please do!'

He took her to the hall and left her there. If her cousin shied away at the notion of having a pregnant young 'criminal', it was better for her not to have a witness.

To Pip, in his living room, he said: 'I hope it comes off. I know you'd rather not be here.'

She coloured. 'It's only ...'

'I know. I let you down. But I couldn't do otherwise, my dear. You're under age to be taken from your family without

134

their consent. Things are different now, of course – they've turned their back on you and you are welcome here.'

'But ... I'd feel more comfortable with Mrs Hawker ...'

'I quite understand.'

Betty came back within five minutes. 'I kept nothing back. I told her all. But we've allus been close, Norah and me, and she just said, "Pick up your bag and come with the lass".'

'That's wonderful!' cried Pip, rather tactlessly but with sincerity.

'Your cousin must be a fine woman,' Hinton said. 'I hope to come and visit her soon. Would that be in order?'

'Oh, you'd be that welcome, vicar.' Betty turned to Pip. 'Is this all your things?'

'Aye.'

'Then we can be gone in no time. Norah told me to get a hire car and she'd pay t'other end. If I could use your phone again, vicar?'

'Feel free.'

Afterwards, as they waited for the car, he tied up some loose ends. 'Mrs Hawker, I don't know if you know it, but the new people staying at Emmerdale for Dolly's wedding are very interested in Steve's case. Mr Ferris is a Q.C., as it happens?'

'Oh aye?'

'He said he'd be willing to act. But because of some legal fussiness, he has to be instructed. Now, as Steve's mother, could you ask Steve's lawyer – the one the court's appointed – to ring Mr Ferris at Emmerdale?'

'You mean ... he'd help Steve?'

'That was most decidedly what he meant.'

'But ... we couldn't afford a Q.C., Mr Hinton!'

Hinton patted her hand. 'There was no question of payment,' he said. 'Now, I hear your car. Let me carry your bag, Pip.'

As he helped them in and waved them farewell, he had a feeling that the future wasn't quite so black for Pip and Steve now. Nothing could wipe out the fact that they had done wrong, but at least society wasn't going to victimise them for ever for one mistake.

He rang Constable Edwards to keep him *au fait* with what had happened, and then Emmerdale. Annie was delighted. 'I've taken the address in Hotten,' she said to Alec afterwards. 'Happen you could drop by? Mrs Hawker told t'vicar she'd hire you or consult you or whatever you call it.'

'She must see Steve's solicitor,' Alec instructed. 'Then he'll get in touch with me.'

'Oh,' Annie was rather dashed. 'You mean you have to hang around waiting for all that?'

'Not at all. I can go and see Mrs Hawker in a purely social capacity. But I can't begin to get together a case for Steve until I'm instructed.' As Annie looked bothered he smiled at her. 'Don't worry. I'll be working, no matter how quiet everything may look on the surface.'

'Vicar said he thought Pip would want to be seeing Steve. Could that be arranged?'

'I think so. I'll go tomorrow and scout things out. Can I ring Mrs Hawker at this place they're staying?'

'Her cousin Norah's – aye – the phone number's with the address.'

'Then I'll arrange that right now, if I may.'

Annie tactfully removed herself from the kitchen while he used the Emmerdale phone. Pip and Mrs Hawker had just that moment arrived at the house; Mrs Hawker was rather breathless at the speed with which help was coming. 'Oh, of course, Mr Ferris. You come whenever you want to. I'm sure Pip would want you to. Isn't that right, Pip?' There was no reply audible to Alec, but Mrs Hawker went on almost at once, 'The sooner the better, she says.'

'Very well. Tomorrow morning then.'

'We'll be expecting you. Thank you, Mr Ferris.'

'And first thing in the morning, will you ring Steve's solicitor and tell him I'll be dropping in at your request? I'll see him after I speak to you.'

'I'll do that.'

Nodding to himself with satisfaction, Alec put down the phone. He went out to the garden, where Annie was chatting with her father. 'That's fixed,' he said.

'I do thank you, Alec . . .'

'Not at all. Now, where's Matt?'

'Matt?' Annie thought for a moment she was still thinking about the case of Steve Hawker, but recovered. Of course, Alec was a relative-by-marriage of Matt's. Quite likely he had something to discuss about the wedding. She knew that Polly Ferris had been writing and ringing round to Matt's

136

cousins, telling them the date of the ceremony. It was quite a surprise to learn that Matt had cousins in Warwickshire and Plymouth. From all that Annie could hear, they all seemed to be planning to come to the wedding.

'He's up on the grazing land to the east of Grey Top,' she said, 'casting an eye over the lambs he let out now the weather's got warmer at last.'

'Grey Top ... that's the crag –'

'And round to the right, past the rocks.'

'I'll take my binoculars. I might see a peregrine.'

She nodded, already thinking ahead to getting tea ready. Alec fetched his glasses and strolled off.

Matt was walking back in time for afternoon milking. He grinned to himself as he saw Alec outlined against the sky, glasses to his eyes, studying a bird in the sky. 'It's a kestrel,' he said.

'Can you see that without binocs? You've got good eyes.'

'Ah, well, y'see, I have them around me all the time. Some little thing about the outline or the way he's flying tells me what he is. But Joe's the one that's the expert. Joe knows where everything nests and hides out.'

'Does he, indeed. I must have a chat with Joe about it. But at the moment, Matt, I'd like to have a word with *you*.'

'Oh?' Matt said. 'Nothing that'll take long, I hope. I've got milking to do.'

'It's a tie, isn't it ... milking.'

'Has to be done. Twice a day.' They fell into step as they made their way down the slope of the fell.

'How will they manage when you're away on honeymoon?'

'Grandad'll help out, and Ma. If worst comes to worst, you can usually get a neighbour to help out. We're used to that in farming.'

'You've made your whole life in farming, of course.'

'Oh aye. It's all I know.'

'And you're partner in Emmerdale Farm Limited?'

'That's right. T'shares were Peggy's at first – then when she died ...' He fell silent.

Alec was perturbed. He hadn't meant to rouse sad memories. He went on quickly, 'Polly asked me to have a word with you. She's been trying to tell you since we first got here and found you, but somehow so much has been going on she's never found the right moment. So I –'

'You what? What's to do?'

'Do you remember your Grandfather Michael at all?'

Matt was surprised at the question. He'd thought Alec was going to speak of relations coming to the wedding – who looked as if they'd prove to be a problem in catering and accommodation. But he gave his mind to Grandfather Michael.

'That was Mum's Dad, wasn't it?' At Alec's nod he continued: 'I think I met him once or twice when I was a nipper. But that's all.'

Alec cleared his throat, fiddled with the case of his glasses. 'He was quite a rich man.'

'Eh?'

'Oh, no millionaire, I don't mean that. But when he died he left something to each of his grandchildren. You'll have gathered from Polly that there are a lot of them!'

Matt laughed. 'Far more than I ever imagined!'

'Now, Matt,' Alec said, looking rather solemn, 'your share of Grandfather Michael's money was the same as everyone else's. But no one knew how to trace you. Advertisements were placed by the lawyers but there was no response ...'

'We-ell,' Matt murmured, 'I'm no great one for reading t'newspapers.'

'I can see you're too busy for browsing through the personal columns,' agreed Alec, 'but the fact is, your share has been sitting there waiting for you to collect it. It's been on deposit a long time and the interest has increased the whole to something in the region of five or six thousand pounds.'

Matt broke stride. He stared at Alec. 'You what?'

'Be a nice little wedding present for you, eh?'

'You're joking!'

'No, I never joke about legal matters, Matt,' Alec said with a grin.

'Five thousand pounds?'

'Give or take.'

'Heck,' Matt murmured. Then, suddenly beaming, 'Oh, wait till I tell Dolly!'

'Er ... Matt ...'

'What?'

'I'd take it easy on that. I'm looking in from the outside, and it seems to me Dolly's a bit overwhelmed what with one thing and another. First you discover a whole family of relations, then her mother disappears, then she reappears with a new husband ... Poor girl, she doesn't know which way is up at the moment.'

They walked on again. Matt thought it over. 'Well,' he said at last, 'one thing's certain. It doesn't matter how many lost relations turn up for t'wedding – I've got the money to pay for their share o' wedding cake, haven't I?'

Alec went to Hotten next day to see Pip and Mrs Hawker. He didn't come back until evening and thus found only Annie indoors, alone.

'Where is everybody?' he inquired.

'Dolly's gone for the last fitting of her dress, Matt's fetching the wedding invitations from the printers, Joe's helping 'vicar tidy up his garden, and Dad's off on some scheme of his own – don't know what.' Annie was ticking them off on her fingers. 'Oh, and your wife's with Dolly, to give an opinion on the length of the skirt.'

'Well, that's all to the good, because what I have to say is confidential. But I think you'd want to know.' He sat down, accepting the tea she silently offered. 'I saw Steve this afternoon. He's very young, Annie.'

'Of course. He's just seventeen.'

'No, I mean he's very young for his age. Nevertheless, he wants to take on his responsibilities. Almost all he could talk about was Pip and the baby.'

'Poor lad,' Annie sighed.

'In the end nothing would satisfy him but I should make application for him to marry Pip –'

'Marry her? But he's in prison!'

'He can be allowed out for the ceremony. It happens.'

'Oh, nay!' cried Annie. 'Poor bairns! Both of them wi' a court appearance hanging over them, and the lad in handcuffs?'

'There's no question of handcuffs. Prison wardens can be very merciful, Annie. Of course there'd be a guard with him, but to the outward eye the wedding will just be like any other.'

'But where? When?'

'As soon as possible, at Hotten Register Office, by special licence,' Alec said. 'I've got the solicitor to get things in motion. His mother has agreed, and as Pip's parents have washed their hands of her the magistrate *in loco parentis* will give permission.'

'So,' Annie said, shaking her head, 'at last they'll achieve what they wanted from the start . . .'

'You could put it that way,' Alec agreed in a sad voice.

The members of the other, happier wedding were converging on the Woolpack. Dolly was pleased with the almost finished look of the dress, Matt was relieved to have the invitations. Annie had said she would write them and get them in the post that night. It was time to have them on their way, for the banns would be read for the third time the day after tomorrow, and then there was only a week to the ceremony.

Dolly's mother and stepfather were already at the Woolpack, enjoying a pre-dinner sherry. They intended to drive on to Connelton for what Leonard described as 'a slap-up meal' at the Feathers. Phyllis beckoned as her daughter came in.

'Well, Dorothy? How's the gown?'

'It's lovely. Aunt Jessie's very pleased, and Polly said it was like something from Bond Street.'

'I should think so too,' Phyllis remarked. 'I wouldn't want my daughter married in a second-rate gown. Now, dear, about the ceremony . . .'

'Everything's settled, Mother,' Dolly said with haste. 'It's too late now to start stirring things up.'

'Stirring things up? What an expression! I only want to finalise this matter of father-of-the-bride.'

'I told you, it's already settled –'

'But Dorothy dear, you can't really prefer Mr Brearley to your own father –'

'Mother, he's not my father!' She glanced quickly at Leonard, who raised owlish eyebrows but seemed unperturbed. 'No offence, Mr Purwick –'

'Leonard, dear. Call me Leonard.'

'But you see, Mr Brearley is set on being the one to give me away.'

'Then you'll have to tell him, Dorothy. Tell him I insist –'

'No, Mother, you tell him!' Dolly interrupted. She really couldn't bear the thought of Amos's disappointment when he heard.

'Very well, I will,' said Mrs Purwick, rising. With determination she made her way to the bar, with Leonard behind her like a small tug following a liner. 'Mr Brearley, may I have a word with you?'

'Eh?' said Amos. 'Oh, aye – go ahead.'

'In private, Mr Brearley.'

Amos glanced about. Business was light, Henry was in attendance, and Dolly had just come in. He could safely leave the bar. 'This way, then,' he said, raising the flap so Mrs Purwick could come behind it to the back room. He was a bit put out when Leonard came too.

'Now, Mr Brearley,' she began, holding up an admonishing finger, 'I gather that Dorothy arranged with you to give her away at the wedding.'

'Yes?' Amos said with apprehension. He'd been dreading this for forty-eight hours.

'That was before my marriage, of course. Things are different now. Dorothy has a father.'

'A stepfather, Mrs Puwick.'

'Purwick,' Phyllis corrected.

'Beg your pardon. Purwick. As I say, Mr Puwick – Purwick – is no relation, really, is he?'

'But neither are you, Mr Brearley –'

'No, that's right. However, it's a matter of style, i'n't it? A man knows when he's right for the job, don't he? And Dolly's told me that as far as she's concerned I'm the one unless I want to back out. And I don't.'

'You don't? But Mr Brearley, my husband –'

'Beggin' your pardon, Mrs Puwick –'

'Purwick,' Phyllis put in automatically.

'Purwick,' Amos amended. 'It's just that I know I'm the right man.' He drew himself to his full height so that he undoubtedly loomed over the short, tubby Leonard Purwick. 'You have to see it from Dolly's point of view,' he said with some self-approval. 'She'd look better coming down the aisle on my arm and ... and ... well, taking one thing with another, I've decided I've a better claim than you, Mr Puwick. So I'm the one that's giving Dolly away.'

The new Mrs Purwick was so accustomed to having her own way that she had no doubt she could shake Amos from his resolution during the coming week. But she should have remembered what happens when an irresistible force meets an immovable object – something has to give. And as the week went by, it dawned on her that she wasn't going to win this one. Amos was going to don his new suit and walk down the aisle to the altar with Dolly.

The traditional events took place. Joe mounted a stag party for Matt to which most of the males of the village came. It was only around ten o'clock that Joe noticed the groom had vanished. Matt had gone out for a walk, finding the jollification too much for him.

Now that the day was almost here, he was filled with vague apprehensions. Memories of his life with Peggy crowded back. He and Peggy had had their ups and downs – quite a lot of downs, it seemed as he cast his mind back. Peggy had been ambitious for him but he'd never lived up to her hopes. Would he disappoint Dolly too?

Tomorrow's ceremony had grown out of all proportion. What he and Dolly had envisaged as a gathering of some six or ten people had turned into a crowd. He'd heard that Polly had contacted eighteen relatives who were coming. Eighteen! It still staggered him when he thought about it: he'd grown so used to thinking of himself as alone in the world except for his friends at Emmerdale.

He walked up through the lanes of Beckindale, passing the church where tomorrow he'd meet Dolly. It was dusk, there was a clouded moon sailing in the sky.

Vicarage Lane ended, he came to the gate to the fields. And there, leaning on the gate, was Dolly.

'Hello, love,' he said. 'What you doing out at this time o' night?'

She turned. 'What about you?' she asked.

'Got a bit much in the Woolpack,' he explained, joining her to lean on the gate.

'It got a bit much at Demdyke too,' she replied. 'Mother and Aunt Jessie were going on and on about details – silver coin to put in my shoe so I'll walk on silver all the rest of my life, something blue, all that kind of thing . . .'

They laughed a little and leaned close together on the wooden bar of the gate.

'Tomorrow this time, we'll be wed,' Matt said.

'Aye.'

He took her hand. 'I'll do all I can to make you happy, love.'

'Same goes for me, Matt.' She let her head fall on his shoulder. 'Oh, to think I came out to have a think, wondering if I could go through with it!'

'Did you?' He stroked her hair. 'Well, I was a bit in two

minds myself as I walked up the lane.'

They let the foolishness of that die away. Then Matt said, 'You're a lovely lass – you know that?'

'You're a lovely feller,' she murmured.

'I love you.'

'And I love you, Matt.'

He tilted up her face to kiss her. After the kiss he murmured, 'It's not long to wait now. I'll be there waiting for you in t'church.'

'I'll be on time, Matt.'

He smiled, holding her near. 'I'm not counting on that – since it's Amos'll be fetching you!'

'Fancy him sticking it out against my mother!'

'Oh, there's more to Amos than we think!'

'I'm glad it's to be him. Things have turned out well, mostly. Even those two poor kids ...'

'D'you know what Alec told me at t'Woolpack? While we're getting wed in Beckindale church, those two will be getting wed in Hotten Registry.'

'No!'

'Aye, so he says. Special licence and everything.'

'Oh, Matt!' She hugged him with sudden fervour. 'Oh, I'm so glad! It's the last shadow lifted! I have a feeling now ... things will go better for them.'

'And was that important?' Matt asked gently.

'Aye, it was. I don't know why, but I felt I couldn't be really happy while they were kept apart. It seemed – unfair.'

'Well, now they'll be man and wife. And so will we – if Amos doesn't send the car off in t'wrong direction from Demdyke tomorrow!'

But Matt had forgotten that though Amos might suffer from wedding nerves, Henry was there to shore him up. Next day Henry got Amos to Demdyke in time even though he was still tying his tie and trying to put his cufflinks in. Amos drew back in startlement when he saw Dolly.

'Bye!' he said. 'Bye! You look a picture ... a real picture!'

The wedding dress was tight-waisted and full-skirted. The stiff fabric shone with a cool lustre. But nothing could outshine Dolly herself, pale, wide-eyed, radiant with happiness.

The others from Demdyke left in their appointed car. Amos was left with Dolly to wait for the bridal limousine. Amos said in a nervous little rush, 'Look all right, do I? Only I don't want to let you down.'

'No danger of that, Mr Brearley,' she said, smiling. 'You as scared as I am?'

'Not a bit! Er ... well ... I'll not deny I've a twitch in me. This is the first time I've ever done this, you see,' he said.

'Well, me too,' said Dolly.

Amos gaped at her. Then he gave a little laugh. 'Well, that's true! Never thought of that!'

The limousine drew up outside the cottage at Demdyke. The chauffeur got out and opened the passenger door. Amos straightened his shoulders, opened the house door, and offered Dolly his arm.

She took it. All at once he stooped and kissed her on the cheek. 'Giver-away's privilege,' he said.

'Why, Amos,' gurgled Dolly, her nervousness vanishing.

She remembered nothing of the drive to church. Her first realisation of the day was when she saw Matt standing by the altar, sturdy, calm, a smile of love and welcome on his face. She walked down the aisle with Amos, tranquil as a vision in her shimmering gown.

'It's going to be all right,' Annie Sugden thought as she watched her come to the altar. 'They make a fine pair. And if ever any man deserved his happiness, it's our Matt.'

Beside her Sam Pearson watched his grandson Joe step forward to act best man. So many generations of Pearsons and Sugdens had stood before the altar of this church ... He felt a tear gather in his eye and was angry with himself. Carrying on like a silly woman! He blinked it back. But it was happiness that dimmed his sight. Happiness for Matt and Dolly.

When the ceremony was over the newly-weds came back down the aisle to the peal of the organ. The photographer was ready with his camera.

But through the crowd slipped a man whom old Sam had summoned after pursuing him all over the dales for the last ten days.

That bringer of good luck – a sweep. He moved to the front of the crowd around Matt and Dolly. Dolly's eyes went wide in surprise and delight.

She offered her cheek. He kissed it.

But she knew she didn't need any good luck charms to be sure she and Matt would be the happiest couple in the dales.